**BLOOD RITUAL: THE ADVENTURES OF
SCARLET AND BRADSHAW, VOLUME 1**

Theodore Roscoe

Champion of Lost Causes

BY MAX BRAND

The City of Stolen Lives: The Adventures
of Peter the Brazen, Volume 1

BY LORING BRENT

The Complete Cabalistic Cases of Semi Dual,
the Occult Detector, Volume 2: 1912–13

BY J.U. GIESY AND JUNIUS B. SMITH

Doan and Carstairs: Their Complete Cases

BY NORBERT DAVIS

The King Who Came Back

BY FRED MacISAAC

The Radio Gun-Runners

BY RALPH MILNE FARLEY

The Scarlet Blade: The Rakehelly Adventures of
Cleve and d'Entreville, Volume 1

BY MURRAY R. MONTGOMERY

Sabotage

BY CLEVE F. ADAMS

South of Fifty-Three

BY JACK BECHDOLT

BLOOD RITUAL

THE ADVENTURES OF SCARLET AND BRADSHAW, VOLUME 1

THEODORE ROSCOE

ALTUS PRESS
2016

EDITED AND DESIGNED BY
Matthew Moring

PUBLISHING HISTORY
"Jungle Joker" originally appeared in the May 1927 issue of *Action Stories* magazine
(Vol. 6, No. 9). "Framed" originally appeared in the June 1927 issue of *Action
Stories* magazine (Vol. 6, No. 10). "Wolves of the Yellow Sea" originally appeared
in the July 1927 issue of *Action Stories* magazine (Vol. 6, No. 11). "The Phantom
Castle of Genghiz Khan" originally appeared in the September 1927 issue of *The
Danger Trail* magazine (Vol. 7, No. 2). "Blood Ritual" originally appeared in the
October 1927 issue of *Action Stories* magazine (Vol. 7, No. 2). "Claws of the
Night" originally appeared in the December 1927 issue of *Action Stories*
magazine (Vol. 7, No. 4). "Sun-Touched" originally appeared in the January 1928
issue of *The Danger Trail* magazine (Vol. 8, No. 3). "The Idol Breaker" originally
appeared in the January 1928 issue of *Action Stories* magazine (Vol. 7, No. 5).
"The Brass Goddess" originally appeared in the March 1928 issue of *Action
Stories* magazine (Vol. 7, No. 7). "Doom Dungeons" originally appeared in the
October 1928 issue of *Action Stories* magazine (Vol. 8, No. 2). "The Thirteenth
Knife" originally appeared in the November 1928 issue of *Action Stories*
magazine (Vol. 8, No. 3). "Scum of the East" originally appeared in the June
1929 issue of *Wild World—Adventure Trails* magazine (Vol. 14, No. 2).

THANKS TO
Everard P. Digges LaTouche and Gerd Pircher

ISBN
978-1-61827-231-7

Visit *altuspress.com* for more books like this.
Printed in the United States of America.

TABLE OF CONTENTS

JUNGLE JOKER

Pretty Dick's twisted features were a mild reflection of his evil heart, but he held all four aces—and the joker!

A WESTERING SUN was dropping behind black jungle when Peter Scarlet, the little American curio-hunter, reached his bungalow. Twilight lay death-quiet over the dark verandah, and the afterglow spread an ethereal pallor in the patch of sandalwood before the door. From the river that crawled through the clearing seeped the fetid stench of stagnant mud, mud that might suddenly creep forward and snap open a long battery of slim teeth. There is something loathsome about a crocodile.

Peter Scarlet was feverish and fatigued. His three day journey into Minang had proved unfruitful. A ride under staggering copper sky had baked the eyes in his head, and the breathless, steamy jungle had almost exhausted his reserve energy. He slid wearily from the pony, and left the animal wandering to its stable.

"Where in hell is that fool boy of mine?" he fretted, when his *kit-mut-gar* failed to appear. "First my coolies fall behind and get mired up for a week. Now my house servant sleeps on the job. What a sweet country this is! I'll beat up that boy again. Lord, it's hot! I'll have to stuff down some more quinine. Lucky if I see at all, then. Damn those trees, anyway! They whisper like lost souls!"

On the verandah he dropped his provision-box, and directed a few of those good round oaths of the sea at the boy whom he guessed to be dozing inside.

Hoping to catch the boy loafing, Scarlet tip-toed to the door and gently pushed it open. As he did so, night drank up the last filtering ray of twilight in a gulp, and flung a burden of darkness over the jungle. Thick darkness. The kind of blackness that can be grabbed between the fingers. It was so sudden and so Stygian and so infernally hushed that it made the little American curio-hunter mighty nervous. He did not enjoy that jungle night.

Nerves tingling, he peered into the silent bungalow. An oath dropped from his lips. The hair rose on the nape of his neck. Gooseflesh quivered on his spine. Staring from the murk that marked the center of the room was a tiny red eye! Biting through the inky gloom it glared like a blood ruby, a single coal of fire. That was what it was.

Peter Scarlet, recovered from the shock, laughed. "Wow! but that's spookey! That cigaret burns like a demon's eye in the darkness. Bradshaw, you give a fellow the chills. Why do you sit smoking in this damned dark room?"

But it was not Bradshaw the friendly naturalist from ten miles up the river. The tone of voice that answered almost threw Peter Scarlet from his feet. It was a hoarse, slovenly, sneering tone, with a peculiar tongue-tied quality, an inflection that told you it came from the thick red neck of a grog-swilling ruffian who had no right to be where he was. It was the angering, domineering drawl of a swashbuckling bully.

Scarlet did not recognize the voice, but he had heard the tone a thousand times. The Port Said sailor who had filched his luggage owned such a voice. So did the rascally skipper on the wallowing bumboat that raided the river ports.

The voice snarled, "Come in stranger, an' make yerself t' home. Nice lil place I got here, huh? If yer th' bonny I think yar come right in! Come peaceful, though, stranger, 'cos I got ya covered."

Peter Scarlet would have given his Providence bank account right then to have had his gun. He would have given his priceless collection of rare Brahman jewelry. He would have given his right eye! But his weapons were on his horse, and his horse was in the stable.

"Who's that?" he demanded, his voice husky with anger. "Who the devil are you? You sure have rare crust being in my bungalow! Get that? *My* bungalow!"

"So?" leered the voice, and the cigaret described a series of arcs in the blackness. "So—so—so! Y' ain't got a gun, w'ich suits me fine! Split me open, pardner, but you ain't holdin' even a face card. Me, pardner, I got me four aces—two fists an' two guns—boot me dead I have! An', b' God, cut my gullet if I don't hold th' joker, too! Lookee, stranger!"

Flaring suddenly, a match lit up the room. Peter Scarlet was a sick man then; almost fainted from nausea. The flickering flame illuminated a countenance too hideous for conception—eyes like blinking block buttons sewed on a sheet of mottled canvas, eyebrows almost meeting hair, scrubby brown bush straggling over gaunt cheeks to bovine jaw. But what caused the mist of horror to clamy on Scarlet's eyelids was the terrible expression lent the visage by a torturous, fresh-cut, burning scar that streaked like a hot wire from under the right eye, smack across the lips to the left side of the drooping chin. A ghastly bit of knife-play, that, screwing the face into a twist of malignant ferocity.

"Well, pardner, I ain't no beauty, eh? Not fer nothin' does they call me Pretty Dick. Pretty Dick Gans, that's me. Some physog, huh?" He gingerly touched his scar. "Got me this in a Singapore gin-battle, and th' Portuguese sailor who done that piece o' whittlin' got his, an' you may lay to that!"

The match glimmered out. The little American, paralysed with dread, shrank in the darkness. Another match sputtered, and he was in hell again.

"Fascinatin' mug I got, I admits," continued the intruder, as the curio-hunter shuddered under his gaze. "An' call me Pretty Dick!" As he chatted he lit a candle on the table. "Yessir, I be him. An' here's my aces!" He swung to sight a pair of ponderous British Army automatics. "Them's trump cards, pardner. Them an' these—" Two massive, hairy stub-fingered hands knotted into fists under the candle-light. The demon face split in a grin. "But hell, ya ain't seen th' card that tops th' deck, yet! Here's a card what takes all tricks, it does!"

Reaching under his chair he found a heavy cord. With a merciless yank he jerked the rope, and from under the table came a savage screech. The next minute another devil ruled hell—the very brother of the corpse-faced Dick Gans; the only creature on earth to share his throne with him.

"Meet Joker," announced the scarred atrocity. "Him's th' damndest an' wickedest an' strongest orang-outang goin'! Give yer face a good stretchin', he could, ya bet y' life!"

PETER SCARLET, the American curio-hunter, had attained the distinction of fifty years at the time of this story. Twenty of those years he had devoted to the Orient with a passion that grew as each sunset painted the sky; and he was no novice in the strange and extraordinary adventures that the ancient lands of the East might stage for him.

A score of terrifying experiences had found him cast in the leading role. He had, with fierce energy, once resisted the damning anguish of a Chinese water-torture. He had survived the horror of being flung into the Ganges amidst a battling mess of foul fanatics—that water just writhed with disease. He had crawled, thirsting, across a frying desert waste, and had spent a screaming afternoon in a Siam jungle at grips with a python as relentless as flying hours to an aged man, as strong as twenty oxen. Small wonder that his hair—little enough on his head but plenty on his chin—had blown a trifle snowy. Yet he remained adamant to the beseeching letters from old friends.

"Come back," they cried, "to America. You old fool, stop this silly trapsing over Asia after bric-a-brac. Why don't you live like a human being? Come back to New York—"

And the little man's sea-blue eyes would twinkle, his bronze cheeks and forehead would wrinkle up in a grin; for paralleling his volcano temper was an equally violent sense of humor.

"Like a human being—" he would laugh. "In New York!"

But he was sorely tempted to return, after that three-day ordeal in the nerve-shattering company of Pretty Dick Gans, his four aces, and the trick-taking top card, the orang-outang, Joker.

Just a glimpse of Dick Gans was enough to appall any man, and his ape was little better, a mangy, offensive, sullen brute with steel muscles and sawlike fangs.

"My pal an' me just dropped in fer a rest," explained Dick in his peculiar voice, eyeing Scarlet along the barrel of his automatic. "We be plenty tired, Joker an' me. I say, shorty, take a chair. Yeh. Step right in an' close th' door. Set down! Fine! Fine business, shorty. Do everything Pretty Dick orders an' you lives. Make a move Dick ain't likin', an' you dies. Say. Supposin' you draws a knife an' stabs me as I sleeps. Know wot? Joker, he's wot. He'd just rip you apart fer that! Ya bet y' wife, he would! 'Cos th' ape keeps a feather eye on Dick. Raise a finger agin me an' Joker'll poke yer ribs in. He ain't lettin' nobody lay a harmin' hand on Dick; be ya, Joker?"

He accompanied the question with a kick that hurled the ape against the wall. The beast screeched curses at its master, but the fear of God was in its eye.

"Ya sees!" continued Pretty Dick, smiling only as such a face could smile. "I got 'im tamed. He's most as scairt of me as you are. An' he hates me most as much. But Joker knows I'm more'n his equal, you betcha! He obeys! Obeys right smart! He sleeps with one peeper open fer anyone harmin' me. An' I sleep with a eye open on Joker. So no harm's done either way, see? Now you! This your outfit?"

Peter Scarlet violently intimated that it was. He also hinted, and not gently, that Dick Gans could take his face and his orang-outang, get out, and go to hell, and that if he did not there were stalwart police in the region to help him.

Dick mockingly returned that possession was not nine-tenths of the law—it was the law! He proceeded to back up his statement by rising to the height of six feet four, and he proved sterling marksmanship by driving bullets into a few of Scarlet's cherished curios that decorated the bungalow wall. As clinch-

ing argument he clipped away the end of the startled curio-
hunter's snowy beard with a neat shot.

Scarlet writhed and sputtered in an agony of fear and fury.
The ape jabbered and mimicked him from its retreat in a corner.
Pretty Dick bellowed with laughter—his laugh was a dread-
fully hollow thing—and dropping his guns into his belt, swung
his feet to the table.

"Tiffin!" he roared. "Jump some food onter this table afore I
tell Joker ta thumb out yer eyes! Don't go runnin' fer no guns
ner knives, er out that door, 'cos th' monk can leap like a stick
o' lightnin'!"

So began three days of exquisite torture for Peter Scarlet.
He found the prostrate form of his *kit-mut-gar* bent double
beside the camp stove. Joker had playfully done that, the "pretty"
one told Scarlet between bites of the *chippatis* that the curio-
hunter had been forced to offer. It was also suggested that one
false step on Scarlet's part, and Joker might toy with Scarlet.

Speechless and horrified, Peter Scarlet watched the boy's
body dragged from the bungalow and tossed into the green
river. Rose a flurried commotion of splashing water and flipping
tails. Mud moved.

"Trot out some rum, an' lively!"

Raging, the little curio-hunter did as he was ordered; praying
only for the intervention of a visitor, or the chance to find a
weapon. But the rack of rifles that had been in the gun-room
had disappeared, and his every move was watched. Joker shambled around at his heels through the rooms, grinning, stinking
fiend with powerful hands that Scarlet knew could crush him
as if he were a bird's egg. Pretty Dick had fastened shut all the
blinds and kept the door closed. Scarlet had not the slightest
chance of bolting.

In two hours the bungalow had been reduced to a shambles.
Pretty Dick flung himself all over the place, wantonly smashing
things up, and occasionally hurling boots and crockery at Joker.
The ape thoroughly enjoyed the fun, and twirled back any

missile that came to hand, until a monsoon might have been
blowing over the American's place.

Like a barroom wench Scarlet slaved and cooked and fed
his two captors, wading miserably about in a heap of trash,
watching apprehensively as the ape, in devilish enjoyment,
wandered from one infamy to another, tearing down tapestries,
smashing dishware, and spilling wreckage over everything.

Pretty Dick sat back and guffawed. Peter Scarlet was scared
sick of him, and he knew it. He knew that the little man was
going mad with horror of him. Dick realized that, and was well
pleased.

Scarlet would have thrown himself at his tormentor, unequal
as that fight would have been, had not it meant certain death
at the hands of the orang-outang.

Dick laughed, for he held every card. No man was ever as
bestial as this Pretty Dick Gans!

Scarlet ached with the hate of him. He lay awake all night
wildly planning escape, tortured by the memory of his captor's
countenance, shivering at the ghastly snores that whistled from
the mutilated face. Peter Scarlet stayed awake. And the orang-
outang stayed awake and watched Peter Scarlet. Pretty Dick
Gans kept a weather eye out for the orang-outang and Peter
Scarlet.

Scarlet would move. The ape would move. Pretty Dick would
move.

Outside the black jungle steamed, weltering under tropic
night, throbbing with the stillness of the catacombs.

PETER SCARLET awoke from a stupor-like doze into living
nightmare. Shrill cries were issuing from the verandah which
was flooded crimson under boiling, morning sun-glow. Dick
was beating his ape. It was not nice. The animal screams were
almost human.

Scarlet could have yelled in frenzy. He scrambled from the
chair in which he had spent the night, and groaned with a
thousand sore muscles. As he gained his feet the screaming ape

fled into the room and bounded under the table, where it crouched, quivering with fear.

Pretty Dick followed. His face was livid, and Scarlet moaned as he saw it. That was not a face. The knobby forehead was boiling with purple veins, and cheeks flushed with drink. The scar disfiguring the mouth was dyed violet.

"Good God!" Scarlet could not restrain the cry.

The renegade whirled on the American. A razor-strap dangled in his hairy fist. With a grunt he drove the leather strap about Scarlet's legs, and Scarlet bawled with pain. *Slash!* It was a barbarous blow, and the little curio-hunter hopped under the smart of it. A cutting lash. It drove terror into Scarlet's heart as it had driven terror into the ape's. But it drove an idea into his mind. That cut from the brutal razor-strap drove an idea into Scarlet's chaotic mind.

He cringed cursing, nursing his blistering ankles, wondering if he would be alive five minutes hence, and striving to capture the fleeting idea. The thought returned. Scarlet wrapped a death clutch around that thin straw of an idea that might save, by the narrowest chance, his life.

Pretty Dick stood glaring at him from savage eyes.

"That's only a warnin' o' wot I might do!" he snarled. "This here Joker fella got funny this mornin' an' bit at me. He hates me. But he's damn scairt o' me!" He snapped the razor-strap with a crack. "He's scairt! An' so are you, shorty. Scairt green, ain't ya?"

Peter Scarlet said nothing. He was fondling his idea.

"All right, shorty. Dig in an' tote out some more rations. Joker an' me's eatin'. Come out!" he shouted at the ape.

The brute sidled out from under the table, to squat before its master. It chewed aimlessly on a bread crust, thumped the floor with its knuckles, and chattered peevishly.

Peter Scarlet knew, and Pretty Dick knew that the ape wanted nothing more than to sink its fangs into Dick's imbecile forehead. And that ape knew it, too. It wanted nothing more in all the world than to destroy this monster of a man who had tamed and tortured it. But Joker's animal heart had been beaten to mash, crushed to submission. The ape dared not resist; dared only to serve. The ape knew that, also. And Pretty Dick knew it; and so did Peter Scarlet.

The razor-strap flicked before Joker's eyes. "See this! Yer gets it every time ya shows yer teeth at me! An' ya gits worse if ya ever let anyone raise a finger agin me!" The beast whimpered. "Come on, pardner! Rush that grub fer Dick an' Joker! Lively, now! Er I'll sic th' monk on ya!"

Boiling with resentment, Scarlet obeyed. He dared not resist. Not yet. So he brought his captor cold *chippatis,* hot tea, and despite his filthy surroundings, managed to eat something, himself. Later in the morning he contrived to sneak down a stiff nobbler of gin, and felt considerably braced.

Not once that day did the little curio-hunter get out of his captor's sight. But he was growing accustomed to Dick's shocking visage, and learned to avoid the ape. He realized that as long as he made no move toward Dick the ape could sense as hostile he was safe from the brute. So he held himself in to play a waiting game.

The bungalow was reduced to complete wreckage that morning by Joker's vagaries.

Peter Scarlet spent the afternoon on the floor playing at dice with his captor. Pretty Dick Gans made him play. He forced the game with the two British Army automatics, and much hardy profanity. Scarlet guessed, and accurately, that the renegade was a deserter from the Indian Army. Sweating, he rolled the dice, and tried to concentrate on his plan.

Dick Gans pulled steadily on a gin bottle. Joker sniffed about the room, examining and smashing articles with monotonous regularity.

Scarlet strove in desperation to think clearly. He must concentrate! But it is difficult to concentrate when one is feverish, squats on the floor in a heap of trash with an ugly orang-outang at one elbow, and two husky automatics at the other—automatics wielded by a creature whose face was simply monstrous in the dim light. And Dick was fondling those army guns all the time. Was he tiring of his game?

A SCALDING yellow moon sailed over the black patch of sandalwood that night, and Peter Scarlet, lying awake watching it through the blinds, wondered if he would ever see it again. Beside him, on a heap of blankets, Pretty Dick Gans snored in animal slumber. Animal slumber—for if Scarlet stirred uneasily one of Dick's eyes would pop open and stare like a shark's eye in the moonlight. Scarlet could see it. The ape was always sighing, and scraping about.

Peter Scarlet was deathly afraid of that beast. He had seen the remains of a naturalist who had ventured argument with an angry orang-outang. There had been difficulty in identifying those remains. Perspiring from every pore, Scarlet fought to control his nerves and lie quiet on the floor. Lying there in the moonlight, listening to his captor's wailing snores and the alert movements of the ape, Scarlet watched the yellow moon rise into the mysterious jungle night sky; and he planned. He planned on the idea suggested by the razor-strapping he had received that morning.

The ape watched him, but could not read his mind.

When the plan had been formulated, Scarlet settled down to pray. Few men could pray as fervently as that little curio-hunter did that night. He prayed with all his heart. With all his soul. Sweat formed on his whispering lips. He called upon all the Saints he knew, and upon some he did not know. The Almighty has seldom been petitioned the way little Peter Scarlet petitioned Him that night. That man prayed!

The sandalwoods murmured accompaniment, and heavy scents from distant jungle land drifted through the blinds....

Peter awoke with a terrified start, horrified that he had slept. Snores at his side, ghostly snores, told him that his captor was still there. With an effort, Scarlet sat up. Came a snarl. The ape watched him with guttural growls. Pretty Dick blinked awake, thumbed his eyes, and yawned. The game was on.

A well-aimed gin bottle sent Joker screaming under the table. Scarlet was glad, seeing the hate sparkle from the ape's eyes.

"Grub!" boomed the renegade. "An' hand out s'more grog! Hustle! Say, little whiskers! I'm damned sick o' yer lazy, careless ways. Look at yer bungalow! Torn all t' hell. Clean 'er up t'day, an' be quick about it!" He staggered from the blankets and kicked them from his boots. "Joker! Hop out here to ole Dick!"

Showing its fangs, the ape ambled from under the table. Pretty Dick brought the beast to time by a vicious tap with the butt of his automatic. Joker stormed, and slunk under the table again.

"Stay there, then!" roared Dick, amiably. "Ner don't come out, ya smelly devil! Haloo, shorty! Where's th' food!"

Scarlet was puttering over the camp stove.

"You'll get it!" he snapped bitterly.

Every minute he spent cooking he would have traded a fortune to have an ounce of poison in the bungalow.

In a trice Dick gobbled down the rice cakes, and tossed a piece of meat under the table.

"There's to ya, Joker! I'll kick off yer brown hide yet. Shorty! Tote out th' rum!"

"I'll get it."

Scarlet darted into the gun room. It was a room that had been the pride of his heart. Now prize pelts, photographs, hunting jackets, helmets, lay in confusion on the floor.

"May that ape squirm in hell for a million years!"

In a corner he located a case of brandy, and grabbed up a bottle. The drunker Dick was, the better.

"Lively there, pardner. Th' ape's got a eye on ya'."

Scarlet sprang to an overturned traveling kit. It was a dusty old kit filled with junk; had been in the bungalow for years. Nervous fingers flew into the bag, and with a "Thank God!"

Scarlet found what he wanted. He found what had been suggested by that razor-strap. An old-fashioned, rusty instrument, relic of Scarlet's youth when whiskers had not been—a nickel-plated straight-edge razor. With quivering fingers he hid it in his shirt and hurried to pour the renegade his drink.

When Dick staggered from his breakfast to the verandah, Peter Scarlet could have whooped with joy. Wildly excited, he began brushing away the dirty, broken crockery, and picking up the myriad articles that the ape had strewn over the room. As he neared the table he fairly shook with anxiety.

The ape watched him from the doorway. Turning his back to the animal, he drew the razor from his shirt, opened the blade, and slid it under the table. It was an extremely long chance—a desperate chance. But Peter Scarlet knew that nothing but an extremely long chance could save him.

WHEN Dick Gans came inside and closed the door Scarlet was fussing over the camp stove. The ape was picking over a heap of shattered crockery.

"Joker!" hissed its master.

The beast looked up fearfully.

Pretty Dick snatched up a chair leg, and advanced towards the ape. Dick was just having fun. He chuckled. He loved to terrify the animal and see it cringe before him. It was good discipline. Scarlet was almost exploding with nerves. Pretty Dick might have noticed his captive fidgeting about, but most people fidgeted when he was near, and he did not notice.

"Joker," he crooned, and whirled the chair leg.

The ape ducked under the table.

Peter Scarlet was almost fainting with agitation. The whole affair played into his scheme. He had noted that every time its master abused it the ape retreated under the table. Thus the plan. The razor-strap had recalled to Scarlet his unused blade. At first he had been tempted to attack his captor, or cut the fiend's throat as he slept. But that meant subsequent battle with Joker, the ape, and Scarlet dared not chance the encounter, for he was a little fellow of slight build, and the ape could have crackled him to jelly despite the razor.

The ape would not let Scarlet approach the renegade, but if Dick should chance to torment it, might not the ape itself attack its cruel master, given an advantage? Scarlet had put the razor within the beast's reach, and now he waited. The animal might do any of a hundred things, or nothing. It might cut its own throat. Scarlet almost wished it would. Or it might battle its tormentor.

Petrified with expectancy, Peter Scarlet watched.

Jabbering under the table, Joker spied the shiney blade, and almost cut a hand apart in clutching at it.

It is doubtful what the outcome would have been had not Pretty Dick tried to settle it.

The ape danced from its retreat, playfully flourishing the bright blade, jibbering with pleasure. Pretty Dick saw the razor, and yelled. The ape waved the instrument. The renegade fought to draw his guns, and backing away, aimed a kick at the brute. For the first time since its capture the ape saw fear in its master's eye. Yes, the ape saw fear, and recognized it!

Pent up hate of two years welled into the savage breast. With a murderous snarl it flew straight at Pretty Dick Gans, landed on his chest, and swept out with the razor, carving a large portion of scalp from the renegade's skull.

Blood pouring into his eyes, Dick fell shrieking and fighting to the floor. When Joker saw that blood he jerked a scream into space that rang in the jungle like a siren—an exultant, fierce cry that sent ten thousand monkeys skipping like mad for concealment!

Zaff! Zaff! The room shook with shrieks. *Zaff!* The blade sliced crisscross over the face that Joker had learned to hate, but had once feared so much. Rivers of blood crawled over the floor. Pretty Dick, kicked, writhed, flung himself about, wrenched, squirmed, and bawled frantically, but the ape clung like glue—clung and carved.

Scarlet had rushed into the gun room, battered out a blind, dived from the bungalow, and raced to hide in the stable. He had hoped to find his carbine and saddle-pistols, but the pony had wandered away. Pale, crouching in the straw, he listened to the crash and cry of combat.

Followed silence. Silence in the bungalow.

Tense with caution, Scarlet crept to peer from the stable door.

He was just in time to see Joker, the ape, fiendishly jabbering, drag a limp, silent, sagging burden from the open gun room casement, and lug it off among the sandalwood trees.

PETER SCARLET, the little American curio-hunter, does not play cards any more. To those who knew him when he loved nothing better than to shirtsleeve a night away hard at a furiously contested poker game his new attitude is decidedly mysterious. Now he never so much as glances at a deck of playing-cards.

And you could not induce him to go back into that jungle south of Minang. Peter Scarlet would not have returned to that jungle for anything, despite his passion for curios. He would not have gone back into that jungle for the pelt of Buddah's tiger, or the whispering rubies of Jehan Jee—no—nor the fabled beard of Mohammed! And those *are* inducements.

FRAMED

*The gods cast Peter Scarlet, Yankee curio
hunter, for the rôle of an avenging fate
in a dark Burmese murder mystery.*

PETER SCARLET RUSHED into the room just as the police were clattering down the shambles of a stairway. Followed a delegation of screeching dance-girls, their painted faces squirming in excitement, and three cursing sailors wholly delighted with the uproar.

Bob Flowerblossom, gaunt and evil proprietor of the Den of a Dozen Joys, came sprinting through one of the many cane-matting doors that led the police only wished they knew where. The Zebu, Flowerblossom's able drink-mixer and cohort of Satan, crept from another door, his big head wagging on the malformed hunch-shoulders that had loaned him his name.

The foul air vibrated with chatter as they stared at a scene peaceful as they were turbulent. In one corner of the drinking-room an aged seaman crouched in his chair. He was exceedingly tranquil. He was dead. One of the bullets had driven into his neck, and the other had, by the looks of the crimson splotch spreading over his jacket, struck home to his heart.

In the opposite corner of the room a young man sprawled head on arm slumberingly, peacefully drunk. His face, stupid with liquor, withered from something worse, ill-shaven, was the face of an old man on the body of a boy. Dirty linen suiting bagged on his shrunken form, tattered as the shapeless shoes on his feet.

Scarlet sickened at the sight of him, but the crowd paid no notice to such details—ragged men in ragged clothes are not extraordinary to the Orient. The crowd's eye was on the pistol that lay on the table under his inert fingers. Gray smoke wisped from the pistol muzzle in slender spiral to join the haze that drifted along the low ceiling. The crowd's eye did not miss that detail. Then it fixed on the man standing at the deserted bar. Here was a tall Englishman in spotless flannel, neat tie, cordovan boots, a panama on which no tropical shower had poured. His fingers played a bit nervous with his yellow moustache, but he surveyed the clamor with a smile of disdainful amusement, and perhaps defiantly under the disconcerting stare, turned to drain his beer mug.

From his place in the jammed doorway, Peter Scarlet watched the Englishman with grave attention, then eyed the drunken boy, And he made up his mind.

Now the police, never losing opportunity to push, jostle and bluster, gained the center of the floor. Notebooks came out. Orders. Questions. Another flurry on the stairs; and a brisk young English Lieutenant of his Majesty's Police was dominating the scene.

One glance pronounced the aged seaman stone dead. The drunken young man was shaken into drowsy consciousness. The Englishman at the bar was wrung in the inquisition of the law.

"Just who else witnessed this shooting?"

Bob Flowerblossom stormed to the fore. His mean face writhed obsequiously. His voice whined shrilly:

"I tell yuh, Cap'n, that none o' my crew has got anythin' to do with it! G'dam it! Seems though somethin' allus happens t' git this here place o' mine in dutch. Here ever'body is peaceful an'—"

"Shut your gab!" roared the young lieutenant furiously.

Peter Scarlet chuckled. He liked to see bravery. It took a brave man to enter Bob Flowerblossom's place and tell him to shut his gab. Scarlet looked from the stern-jawed young policeman to the lobbing drunkard at the table. The officer continued:

"An' don't open that trap again except to answer my questions. We all know what a quiet, peaceful little church you run here, Flowerblossom. Don't waste your breath tellin' us what a benevolence you are to the community. We know that already. By God, Bob, if there's one thing I'd like to do while I'm stationed here it would be close up this rat hole! Now, who saw the shooting? Did you? No? Then say so! How about the ladies?"

"We was all dancin' to th' tin pianer in th' back room, Chief," hiccoughed one of the sailors.

"Yeh!" chorused the others.

"Hell!" snarled the lieutenant in icy sarcasm. "I suppose nobody saw it an' nobody did it. Have I got to take you all in? Now, here—"

"Just a moment, bobby!" It was the Englishman who had been standing at the bar. He pushed up to the policeman, "I can help you. I was here when it happened. That mob had nothing to do with it, and if you'd clear most of them out—"

Most of them were cleared out, under guard. Bob Flowerblossom, Zebu, and Peter Scarlet remained where they stood.

"What do you know, sir?" the lieutenant had demanded of the curio-hunter.

"The boy at the table, there," Scarlet admitted. "An acquaintance. I didn't see the affair, but perhaps I can lend a hand."

"All right, glad for a little Christian help. Now, sir, you saw it. What occurred?"

"The Englishman straightened his tie.

"This fellow," he explained, "had just drawn my beer, and left through the door over there." He nodded at the hunch-backed dwarf, and indicated a door near the bar. "No one else was in the room except myself, that old seaman, and the drunk." He pointed to the dead sailor, and the boy at the table, who had sunk into alcoholic stupor again. "Briefly, all I know is that the two men were seated as they are now. I had just come in. My back was turned. The gun fired twice. A beastly racket. I jumped around—" He waved a hand at the murdered seaman. "And there you have it. That's all I know about it, bobby. The rest seems pretty evident."

With a sniff the lieutenant picked up the pistol from the table. "Two shots; righto."

Grabbing the drunken sleeper, he shook him violently.

"Slopped," was his disgusted snort. "Goin' out cold. Probably hardly knew he fired those shots. So you know him, do you?" he asked Scarlet.

"A young construction engineer," Scarlet replied. "I only know him slightly. Some of my friends knew him well. A regular fellow, a while back. Looks as if he hadn't stood the gaff."

The Englishman volunteered: "If he is young Herdon Scotts, I, myself, have heard friends speak of him in London. They said he was out here. But this beggar can't be him!"

"Well, he's passed out now. Likely he won't recall a thing about it. Poor devil, he's in for it. Looks as though he's well doped, too. The dream pipe. Seems to get a lot of them out here. Well, Sher Baz! Tote that stiff out to the wagon, then come back and help me with this lad. And now, gentlemen, give me your names, and kindly come with me to headquarters. Jolly sorry to bother you. And you, Flowerblossom! Bring that bloody henchman of yours with you, and show up at the Chief's this afternoon, or we'll raise hell with you. This is your third tea-party this month, an' maybe somethin' will be done about it."

Nothing was done about it, which proved to Scarlet that the American law machines are not the only ones with crippled gearing somewhere. Bob Flowerblossom ducked and cringed and perjured, and returned to his hole grinning. The atrocious Zebu perjured and cringed and ducked, and went with him.

The trial was short. It was held on an incredibly hot day. The stench from the native quarter enveloped the entire town. The judge was suffering with jungle fever, his head buzzed with quinine, and the last thing on earth he wanted to do was hold court. Testimony was given quickly. The Englishman proved to be one Sir Wallack Welch of London, on business for his father, a pearl-buyer; going to be stationed in the town for the next two years. He had heard of the accused from a party in London, but did not know him. He described the shooting. Peter Scarlet simply testified to the identity of the accused.

The accused, Herndon Scotts of London, on location for the United Kingdom Foundation Co., was doing construction engineering on a dam for the Irrawaddy River. No, he did *not* murder the old seaman! His lips moved in incessant denial of guilt. He did not recall the affair. With difficulty they made him understand he was on trial for murder. He hardly comprehended. He had never seen the gun before. He didn't give a damn about the whole damn business, and they were jolly bounders not to give him just a touch of—of—No! *damn* it! He had never owned that pistol.

Herndon Scotts squirmed and writhed, sick, shivering, wretched, his body screaming for drugs. Firmly he denied guilt. Why should he kill the sailor, and how could he when he never carried that gun? All he wanted was a drink. A smoke.

He wept.

The judge was annoyed. This was going to disturb everything; might drag the trial a month.

Then Bob Flowerblossom kindly helped things along. He testified that he had been sitting in a back room. Which back room? What did it matter ——there were many back rooms. At any rate he had heard quarreling. He had paid no attention to it, he heard a lot of it. But it certainly was the young engineer's voice.

"You're a damn liar, an' I wanna drink!" mumbled the accused without enthusiasm.

"Chief," protested Flowerblossom, "that's Gawd's truth as I swore on th' Bible."

He established it as God's truth, himself as a veritable missionary to the district, and his Den of a Dozen Joys, a holy shrine and decided benefit to the town. He got a reprimand from the judge for talking so much; the jury was out three minutes; and Herndon Scotts got seven years for murder while intoxicated.

Peter Scarlet watched him as he was hauled weeping and twitching and blubbering away to prison. He also watched the smile under the yellow mustache of the English pearl-buyer's son. Thereafter he voiced a good pink American oath, washed it down with red rum, and retired to his hotel room, where he could smoke one of his lethal cigars and scratch off a letter in peace. The letter was bound for London.

DURING the following months, Peter Scarlet, the little American curio-hunter, was unusually busy. Report of silver plates inscribed with minute chapters of the Zend-Avesta lured him panting to the Persian border. He failed to locate the mysterious plates.

On returning to the town he called in on the Den of a Dozen Joys several times, ostensibly for a lug of brandy, but actually to see what was going on. What he saw there evidently pleased him.

Later, he dashed over to Assam after gavial skins, from there to Calcutta, thence to Yezo, where he obtained some admirable Japanese prints and back to Singapore, where the admirable Japanese prints were stolen. When he finally returned to town his post-box was flooded with letters. Some of the envelopes were legal envelopes. And some were scented blue.

Meantime the Burmese law courts had been prodded into activity. Scarlet watched in interest as the case of Herndon Scotts was again dragged over the books, and he gave his own testimony with others until it was established that the young engineer had been sentenced on too thin evidence. No one had actually seen him fire the shot. It was proved that he had no reason for quarrel with the victim. And the fact that he was dead drunk weighed heavily in his favor; it was highly improbable that a drunkard's shooting had planted those bullets so neatly in the neck and heart of the old seaman.

Twenty-one months after his imprisonment, Herndon Scotts left the Rangoon prison. If Scarlet had been busy during those months, so had Scotts. Very busy, indeed. The young man's hands were tough with callouses. He knew a pick-axe when he saw one. In his eyes was a thoughtful look. Sullen, perhaps, yet thoughtful. Evenings behind gray walls, after he had recovered from the violent illness of his early confinement, had given him time to think, and to recall.

Peter Scarlet encountered Herndon Scotts on the veranda of the Queen Mary House two days after the engineer's release. Scarlet hardly recognized him. Trimly clad, he was, in clean linen, new leather boots, a *topee* with a wide white band. His face wore a peculiar expression, but not the withered, scared, haunted look of the dope addict who had sprawled in Bob Flowerblossom's gin mill. It was a tanned face and a rugged face—for convict duty on prison roads either kills or hardens. Herndon Scotts looked hardened, Scarlet noted. His shoulders were set as was his jaw. He lifted up his feet. A grimness about his eyes, though, Scarlet did not like. Nor did he like the way Scotts' coat-pocket sagged so heavily.

"Hello there, Scotts," was his genial greeting. "How've you been? Looking fit."

The other swung about; glared keenly at the American.

"Why—you were at the trial weren't you? Scarlet, isn't it?"

"Peter Scarlet," acknowledged the curio-hunter, extending his hand.

Scotts hesitated, then grasped it. His grip was hard and painful. Peter Scarlet grinned.

"Some grip, fellow! Want to kill me? I—"

"Listen," Scotts cut in abruptly. "Will you come up to my room? I'd like to talk to you for a minute. I don't believe you know anything about it, but I'd like to ask a question. Mind?"

In his room the engineer hunched stiffly on the bed, waving the chair to his guest. At once he plunged into conversation.

"Now, sir, I've been two years in prison as you possibly know. I don't give a jolly damn whether you believe it or not, but I was framed, see? Framed!" His brow contracted in a fierce and black frown. His jaw clamped trap-like over the word, "Framed!"

"Sure," agreed Scarlet cheerfully. "You were framed."

"Glad somebody else thought so!" snarled the young man bitterly. "And let me tell you, sir, that I know the bloody rotter who framed me. It was that fox-faced bounder Wallack Welch, or I'm a liar! Come! Do you think so?"

"His idea," chuckled Scarlet. "Listen. That Englishman *did* frame you. I happened to find out why. He was in love with a friend of yours when he left London. She asked him to look you up when he came out here. He found you in the gin mill, and railroaded you to jail to disgrace you with her. We have it all figured out, Carol and I."

"Carol! You know Carol? You know her? She knows? Sir Wallack framed me? I'm disgraced! I know it! I'll kill him! I'll murder him! I've bought a gun!" He jerked an automatic from his pocket. "I'll grind that rotter's face with bullets when I see him! Framed! I'll find him—kill him! Two years. My God! Carol! Where is she? Where is he?

"Dry up!" snapped Scarlet sourly. "Put away that gun. Don't act like a kid. Let me tell you something interesting. I saw the whole murder. Had just stepped into the room from those stairs when the shots were fired. It all happened in a moment. Zebu, the hunchback, shot and killed that sailor. I saw him. He dropped the gun at Sir Wallack's feet and ducked behind a curtain. Nobody saw me on the stairs. Acting like sixty, Sir Wallack snatched up that gun and laid it in your hand—you were dopey at the table. Sir Wallack never would have dared expose the Zebu, didn't dare let the gun lie at his feet, and had an excellent chance to get rid of you. And—"

"I knew it! The rotter! Zebu killed him! Sir Wallack framed me! You saw it! *You!* And you let me go to prison? Why, you dirty stinkin' boun—" His voice rose to a scream. His face ebbed white with madness.

"Shut up!" shouted Peter Scarlet, suddenly angry. "You bet I let you go to prison, you damned kid! Best thing that ever happened to you! You oughta be mighty damned glad! Cured you of booze. Straightened your shoulders. Tanned your mug. Put some muscle on your skinny hide. You got some sleep. You got some time to think over what a mighty rotten ass you'd been—untrue to your little girl back home. It cured you of the vilest habit known to man, and you know it—that happy smoke had you bad! Suppose your girl had seen that? That's why I let them frame you to jail."

"What right—"

"What right?" Peter Scarlet fairly wriggled in fury. "What right, you young sap! You fool! The right of an old man who doesn't give a damn whether people think he's nosey in their affairs or not! I don't care what anyone thinks of me. Not a damn. Too old! When a man is sixty he does things independently. That's the right I have! I've been all over. Seen a million people, done a million things. Know more in a minute than your young damn generation may ever know. Say, I'd been watching you. Going to hell, you were. Fast! Forgetting your girl and your work. I've seen too many boobs who didn't have the guts to stay decent once they hit an out-trail. Minute they get lonely or tired they hit the grog or the joy medicines. No guts. Make me sick! I didn't want to see it again. I let 'em send you up; let Zebu get away with his murder. The old codger he killed was about ready to check in anyway. As for Zebu, Flowerblossom killed *him* couple months ago. Police didn't even investigate—"

"But Wallack and Carol! He lied to her! He let her think— I'll kill that—"

"Applesauce, as they say in America. You won't do any such thing, Scotts. Flowerblossom's beating you to it. He's near done it by now. If you go down to the Dozen Joys right now, I wager you'll see Sir Wallack. You can't kill him when he's dyin'! His face is screwed up and twitchy, and unshaved. His clothes are ragged, dirty and torn. He's barefoot. He's in a stupor. He's dopey. His mind is shot to hell. Done it all by himself, too. Almost as damn a fool as Herndon Scotts was two years ago!"

Thick, feeling silence followed Scarlet's angry words; silence unbroken save by a paraqueet raging in a nearby tree, the lowing of a water buffalo, and a sighing breeze from the bay. In the distance a temple bell tinkled softly. Sunshine flooding from behind a cloud slanted through the rattan blinds and dropped a pattern of gold on the carpet matting. Sunbeams glinted gold on the bowed head of the engineer, and on the automatic lying in the corner where he had tossed it.

The little American curio-hunter lay back quietly in his chair, silent, with an occasional thoughtful tug at his short, snowy beard. He seemed to be listening.

The gold pattern had moved slowly across the floor of the darkening room, and soft shadows were creeping along the walls when the young engineer rose, opened the blinds, and stared, wordless, out of the window.

Before his eyes shimmered the bay, glorious under the crimson banners of sunset. Twilight danced over the restless blue water, painted the crazy sampans with fantastic shades, and hung the verdant tropical shore with misty violet-tinted dusk. A wisp of smoke from some steamer lingered a thin black haze against the red-dyed horizon.

There was a strange glistening in Scotts' eyes when he turned to face Peter Scarlet.

"I *am* a damned rotter," he whispered. "Carol, I—I deserved to lose her. Carol— Carol— I'm sorry. A rotter— Scarlet, you've been awfully fine. A prince. I can't repay you. Oh, Carol—"

He choked, and bowed his head on the window ledge. Peter Scarlet shuffled uneasily. Horizon fading rose, the sunset's beauty over the boy, his repentance, wrenched the little curio-hunter as he had been seldom moved before.

Far away over the water sounded the throaty signal of a steamer, its echo dying in the jungle.

"Brush your hair, Scotts," Scarlet commanded, fishing energetically in his pocket for a cigar so that the boy might not sense his own emotion. "We might take a stroll down to the wharf. That's the Calcutta mail boat. Docks in half an hour. If I'm not mistaken, Carol's last letter said she'd arrive on that steamer."

The Mysterious East

Framed is another cracking Peter Scarlet yarn laid in that strange, eerie land of the monsoon where white blood shows its weak strain in all too many sad cases. Theodore Roscoe knows his land.

To me, my mother's youngest brother was a most fascinating character. And could he weave a yarn? Who couldn't, had they been born in the heart of India and spent a lively youth adventuring over the Hymalayas—a captain in the English Volunteers at twenty-one.

Framed built itself from the colorful career of one of his companions. The story just lent itself to Peter Scarlet—a disguised acquaintance of my father's—and as for the doped and dissolute Herndon Scotts, he may hit so close to home that someone will be thumping mad.

Perhaps the reader will not think Scarlet justified in meddling with another's affairs, but the curio-hunter's frosty beard has come through a good deal in life, and a man who smokes deadly coal-black cigars can usually get away with anything. As it evolved he was right. I might tell you of a smart engineer who drives a smart car loaded with a smart family—but that's way ahead of the story.

THEODORE ROSCOE

WOLVES OF THE YELLOW SEA

Pigs, pirates, pearls and Peter Scarlet—
on the roaring China Sea.

LOUD, ANGRY VOICES rattled violently in the sultry heat of mid-afternoon. Peter Scarlet lurched awake from his doze on the torrid afterdeck of the *Lotus Flower*. The voices rose strident and quarrelsome.

"Now fellow, you've simply got to do something about those damned pigs!"

Reply came gruff: harsh as sandpaper. The curio-hunter recognized the voice as that of Ogle Bill, one-eyed skipper of the *Lotus Flower*.

"Them hawgs stays! If you blokes is too good ter ship with pigs, w'y I guess yuh c'n wait fer th' mail boat wot touches here three days after t'morrow!"

"That's a confounded outrage! I can't stay another day in this hole. We've paid our passage on your boat. And my wife and friend, here, have not got to sail with a load of stinking swine! Why didn't you say this was a cattle-boat?"

"Tain't a cattle-boat! Wot's more, th' *Lotus Flower* sails in half uh hour, an' them pigs stays where they be!"

"Can't you take them off the deck, then, and stick them in the hold?"

"Ain't no room in the hold."

"Who owns them?"

"He be right aboard, gents, an' yuh c'n talk t' him. Little guy, he is, in w'ite ducks an' a beard. A-sittin' aft there."

Around the corner of the deckhouse stormed the argument. Peter Scarlet stared in drowsy amusement at a tall gentleman perfect in white flannels and spotless helmet. He furiously twirled his monocle, as from his smooth-shaven lips sputtered a speech of protest. He was followed by a pudgy little lady in glowing starchy white dress, her prim head and tilted nose ducking under a sunshade. Behind her lounged a perfect counterpart of the first gentleman, but for a tea-stained yellow mustache. At his side chattered a Malay sailor, and bringing up the rear swaggered Ogle Bill.

The faces of the tall gentlemen were crimson with heat and annoyance. Ogle Bill blinked his solitary eye, and twitched a thumb at Peter Scarlet.

"Say. These here two is pearl buyers, an' their wife who wants passage t' Singapore. Ain't no other craft clearin' from here fer four days, an' these insists that them hawgs o' yours ain't fit smellin' travelin' company. They wants 'em bilked back on shore. Wot yuh say?"

Peter Scarlet passed a handkerchief over his glistening bald head. Fumbling for a cigar, he said:

"Too hot to argue over a small thing like that. I'm sorry, gentlemen, but I came way over here for those pigs, and it's necessary that I take them back with me. There's no other place for their crates than forward there. I came way up here to get them for a research camp of mine."

"But God save us!" exclaimed the mustached gentleman. "Here we are on a little two-by-four excuse for a Chinese junk, barely room enough to walk about as it is, and almost all of the forward deck crammed with crates of dirty pigs! We've paid our passage for the trip, and—"

The curio-hunter abandoned his tarpaulin hammock and made his way forward, followed by the steaming pearl buyers, the starchy lady and the growling skipper. He halted at the side of two big crates lashed to the deck. These crates housed two dozen of the smallest, skinniest, scrawniest, runtiest pigs one could ever hope to see. At Scarlet's approach they set up a shrill squealing and grunting; poked long snouts through the crate bars; black pigs, spotted pigs, brown pigs—all gaunt and unhappy.

The lady in starchy white shuddered. Peter Scarlet grinned.

"I came a long way for these specimens—came myself to see that I got 'em. Awfully sorry, but their passage is paid too; and here they stay. Anyway, after you get out to sea you won't notice 'em."

The pearl buyers snarled, the lady made remarks about the entire country being filthy, and they ordered a coolie to bring aboard their luggage.

"We'll sail, I suppose. No other way out of it. But the confounded pigs will—"

"Suit yersel'," interrupted Ogle Bill, deftly urging a brown jet of tobacco-juice into an open hatch that disclosed the hold loaded with bamboo. "Suit yersel'. Reckon if th' pigs c'n stand it you can!"

No arguing with the one-eyed skipper. Sniffing and grumbling, the passengers clambered to their quarters below. Peter Scarlet returned to his tarpaulin hammock and his cigar. And with canvas billowing, yards taut, and much pungent profanity from its skipper, the *Lotus Flower* headed into the restless blue of the China Sea.

AFZUL AMEER of the Red Turban knew many things. Behind his bulging olive forehead and wicked little eyes was stored a vast knowledge about ships and seas and cargoes and captains. Foremost in his mind, among other potent truths, was the axiom that dead men tell no tales. This he believed with all his heart. And from the Arabian Sea to the Formosa Channel the waters were spotted with the blood of Afzul's victims.

A recent fact of his learning was the whispered information that the *Lotus Flower* under Ogle Bill was about to clear from a port south of Cape Padaran for Mandalay. He knew that two pearl buyers were sailing on the craft. And he knew that those pearl buyers carried a box of black pearls that would buy prayer rugs enough to reach from Mecca to Paradise.

Devout Mohammedan that he was, Afzul Ameer of the Red Turban faced toward Mecca and prayed Allah to blow a little breeze that might send the *Lotus Flower* his way. Whereupon he whipped his Arab pirates into activity. Dirks, knives and daggers were ground sharp, rifles loaded, sails trimmed; and Afzul's ragged lugger cruised the China Sea, peaceful of exterior, but mighty evil below decks.

In his cabin Afzul Ameer of the Red Turban held conference with his mate. Putting bearded heads together they planned the campaign with greatest care. They planned to cope with rare opposition from Ogle Bill, whose fierce dishonesty was only matched by his ferocious honesty, and whose peerless knife-play was touted in many an Asiatic port. It was told of Ogle Bill that his right arm was stout as a mast. Legend had it that he had snapped an axe-handle over that arm. Certain it was that many an opponent had dropped under its powerful drive.

Yes, Afzul owned a particularly keen blade for the skipper of the *Lotus Flower*. And the pirates counted on a joyous battle with Ogle Bill's crew. It was a wild crew that would sign under the one-eyed skipper; a crew that would rather fight than drink. But Afzul's lusty Arabs had slain wilder crews than Ogle Bill's.

Given Allah's blessing, the prize should well be won. All was in readiness.

With satisfied grunts and satisfied sighs the two old villains abandoned themselves to contemplation of the silks, slaves, wines, and women a box of black pearls would buy.

ALLAH answered Afzul's prayer.

The gentle breeze he sent gained the impetus of a hurricane, caught the *Lotus Flower* south of Bishop's Shoal and beat her wallowing and floundering down to the Natunas. Ogle Bill swore green oaths as the tempest snatched away hatches, companions, and sail cloth. Afterward the one-eyed skipper raged to his Chinese mate:

"Only G'damn thing left aboard is them lousy crates o'half-drowned hawgs! Why th'hell wasn't they washed away, an'them lily-livered pearl buyers along with 'em? An'th'fat little stuck-up woman, too! All three is hollerin'sick in their bunks. If they yells much more about this trip I'll slit 'em up an'dump 'em ov'board!

"That there Yankee runt ain't such a swab. Hopped inter some oil-skins, he did, an'lent a hand. See that he gits treated above-board. He ain't such a lubber as the others. Rather carry th'little runt an'his pigs than them tall swabs an'their pearls. Got arf an'eye t'cop their pearls at that! No! No, we don't, Chink! We ain't no pirates yet! We signed t'carry 'em, an'we'll see it through!"

Beaten and badly wrenched the *Lotus Flower* outrode the gale, hauled in her sea anchor, and set nose for Singapore. Below decks Messrs. Worthing and Meade, the pearl buyers, lay in their stuffy cabins, squirming in the ghastly grip of seasickness. Plump Madam Worthing was no longer starchy. She wilted in her bunk, an inert mass of ill, her whines of complaint ever rising against the awful accommodations of the *Lotus Flower*, against the awful-looking captain, against the foul cargo of pigs, and against the curio-hunter who certainly was no gentleman.

As for Peter Scarlet, he had enjoyed the storm. Donning a sou'wester, he had fought to keep himself and his pigs aboard ship. They had not been driven as far from their course as he had feared. He had dried out his cigars, and was cheerful.

Now he lounged against a stern rail, watching with supreme satisfaction the sun as it dropped like a giant red wheel into a tumble of clouds over the distant Borneo shore. Soft warm winds from the Java Sea brushed over the *Lotus Flower;* bellied her drying sail. Water bubbled melody about her rudder, churning a frothy surge in her wake. Tight yards twanged in the wind. The old craft's warping timbers squeaked pleasantly as she wallowed along. Forward rasped a harsh command. Came a pattering of bare feet, the busy rapping of a hammer repairing the gale's damage. Blue was the sea, blue was the sky, and blue was the smoke from Peter Scarlet's cigar.

Sighing in content, he fell into dreamy reverie of strange ports. Memory carried him to Bombay, Mascat, Aden, Port Said, Tunis—all the way to New York. All the way to old Providence. Farther, to a long-gone fireside in an old Southern home where a little Peter Scarlet had dropped his volume of Marco Polo, gazed into crackling flames, and yearned for uncharted seas. Forgotten was his research camp, the *Lotus Flower,* the snobby pearl buyers, his cigar—

"*Yow!*"

Scarlet's senses flung into the present. His hand flew to his hip.

Commotion banged on the forward deck. Ogle Bill was hurling commands. Sailors were scampering for the rigging.

The curio-hunter hurried past the deckhouse, and his blue eyes twinkled with surprise. Heeling in the stiff breeze, a low, crazy craft was plunging head-on toward the *Lotus Flower.* From his position aft Scarlet had not been able to notice the vessel's approach. He saw that it must have slipped from behind a distant island. In the fading afternoon light it loomed fantastic and fast. What made the curio-hunter gape in amazement was the ancient brass cannon that frowned on the high prow of the stranger craft.

"Now blast me!" he breathed. "And I thought all the pirates had joined the movies! Hey!" he shouted to Ogle Bill—the skipper was dashing about, beside himself with excitement— "Hey! Who is it?"

"Looks t'be Afzul Ameer!" screamed the skipper. "Tryin' ter ram us!" He exploded in pungent profanity.

On came the stranger. It seemed as if the *Lotus Flower*, crowding all sail, could not evade her. Peter Scarlet stared in dismay at a row of grim faces peering from the stranger's rail. He caught the shimmer of steel, the glint of gunmetal. The crew of the *Lotus Flower* was blossoming out with sword, knife and gun.

Scarlet fled to his cabin for his repeating rifle. In the companionway he encountered one of the sick pearl buyers.

"I say!" came the peevish query. "What's all the bloody racket over? My wife just dozing off, too. Curse it, what's the matter?"

"Get a move on!" snapped Scarlet. "Quick! Hide your wife or she'll doze for good! Grab a gun! Get your friend! Got valuables with you? Pearls? My God, hide 'em! Pirates! Hurry!"

And he sprinted up the steps, leaving the pearl buyer paralyzed with surprise. On deck again, he found himself in the midst of wild clamor. The Malay sailors were brandishing villainous-looking knives. The Chinese mate waited patiently at his wheel, a heavy musket in the crotch of his free arm. Dancing up and down the roof of the deckhouse was Ogle Bill.

"A fight!" he squalled exultantly at Peter Scarlet. His lone eye shone like a star. He waved a tremendous sword in one hand, a black revolver in the other. A joyous laugh rang on his lips. Off came his shirt. Ropes of muscle played over his tattooed chest. "A fight! A fight!"

"The passengers!" wailed Scarlet.

"T'ell with 'em!" screamed the skipper. "They're best off below! Get ham-strung up here! Hide their ole woman! You tol' 'em?

Good! Come up here aside me with yer guns! We'll leave my lads cut up th' deck! Ha—"

Roar and a flash! The stranger's brass cannon belched smoke. A spar clattered to the deck of the *Lotus Flower*.

"They can't shoot much!" chortled Ogle Bill. "Or they'll have a hundred craft out here. Just tryin' t' cripple our gear. With that Afzul Ameer we got a red hot scrap on our hands! Afzul ain't no lubber! Hi!"

Shots rattled fast as the two ships drew together. With a rending smash the pirate struck the *Lotus Flower* astern. The ship shivered under the blow. The jar ripped away her rudder, and the old vessel ducked to her scuppers. Scarlet was thrown to his face.

As the vessels scraped sides a small army of brown and naked men flourishing weapons dropped from the stranger's rail to the deck of the *Lotus Flower*. Clash was immediate.

Smoke of combat clung so thick that the curio-hunter could only make out a swirling chaos of gleaming arms, glinting knives, and spurting guns. At his side Ogle Bill's revolver flamed. His own automatic jumped in his hand, and grew warm.

"Fight!" bellowed the skipper, his voice hoarse with frenzy.

Those Malay sailors of his fought! The din was intense. Scarlet caught a momentary glimpse of the Chinese mate, his face a mask under blood, whirling his heavy sabre like a maniac.

The screams of the Malays and the Arab pirates, the drifting smoke, the splashes of crimson that began to appear on the deck, pungent powder smell, clang of knife on knife, boiled fighting blood in the little American's veins. He settled down to business. His repeating rifle stuttered a steady bang, spat a river of lead as he sprayed the deck of the pirate craft. Sweat streamed down his face. The gun barrel grew hot. His ears sang with the oaths of Ogle Bill. His moist eyes could see the Chinese mate where he now lay dead, sprawled over a hatch.

Like demons those Malays fought! But the Arabs swarmed aboard like ants. Slowly Ogle Bill's crew was being forced to the forward deck. What seemed like hours to Scarlet was in reality minutes when the savage Arabs had slashed down half their opponents. The after deck was strewn with dead, the timbers slippery under foot. Battle raged amidships.

So valiantly had the crew of the *Lotus Flower* defended her that Afzul's entire band now scrambled aboard, intent on finishing the fight with one fierce swoop. Arab faces grinned up at Scarlet. He grinned back, and his rifle talked.

A dirk nicked his ear. Bullets hummed about him. One shot plugged into his pith helmet, and the cords of his jaw tightened like thongs. Hearing a squawk at his side, he knew that Ogle Bill had been hit. But the black revolver did not hesitate its fire.

The heart of the pirate fighting centered about a tall Arab with criss-cross scars marring his face, a thick brown beard, and lightning eyes—eyes that darted from under a bulk of red turban. His powerful arms swung a sword that might have been Excalibur. Afzul Ameer, himself!

Ogle Bill bawled his identity into Peter Scarlet's ear, and the curio-hunter directed a hail of shot at the lofty figure. Afzul's life seemed charmed. The curio-hunter's bullets flew like rain, and yet the Arab pirate remained unscathed. His men rallied under his dynamic energy. The Malays retreated to the steps leading to the forward deck.

Raging like a fiend Ogle Bill swung into the rigging, to drop like a cannon-shot into the heart of battle. Peter Scarlet followed, fighting in a very hell of knife thrusts and zinging bullets. A sword gaffed his wrist. Grimacing in pain he swung his gun-butt. The pirates surged forward.

Followed a mad swirl of battle. Down went several Malays. Down went Ogle Bill without the major portion of his left cheek. Down went the little curio-hunter. He slid on the red-wet deck, his gun was wrenched from his hands, a knife sliced the calf of his leg, and a sword thrust ruined his beard by trimming away too much from the end.

Falling flat, he spraddled before one of the pig crates. Like wolves the pirates flung themselves upon him. He found himself scratching at a bulging olive forehead. He glared into gimlet Arab eyes. He was clawing at the face of Afzul, the Arab leader.

Like lightning came an idea! He squirmed under the tangle of bodies, kicked out, and knocked the latch from the door of the pig crates.

Something happened. Afzul Ameer of the Red Turban voiced a screech that should have echoed in the Borneo hills. Arab pirates fell back in frantic retreat. Brown bodies plunged into the sea, as over the deck of the *Lotus Flower* poured a terrified squad of little pigs, rushing pell-mell, all squealing like mad.

A skinny black pig had fled over Afzul Ameer's face. Three more had raced over his chest. *Pig! Pig!* Hated curse of the Mohammedan, Allah must have turned against him and his misdeeds.

Afzul Ameer of the Red Turban dove over the rail. His Arab pirates simply lost control. In two minutes the forward deck was alive with pigs, but deserted of pirates.

With wild shouts the Malays lost no time in snatching up weapons and rushing to the rail. One dashed to cut away the hawser tying the *Lotus Flower* to the pirate ship.

Peter Scarlet gained his feet. His automatic heated in his hand. The pirate route was complete. One by one the splashing Arabs sank under the waves.

The last shot was a difficult one, for the vessels had drifted apart. The escaping swimmer had reached the pirate ship, scrambled up the ladder, and gained the deck. But Peter Scarlet picked him off.

In the fading twilight Scarlet might have missed him had he not been wearing a red turban that made a perfect target under a dying ray of sunlight—a turban that sank in a sea flooded with shimmering sunset glow.

"**NEVER** heard anything like it in my life!" complained Bradshaw, the naturalist.

It was five days and forty cigars later. They were sitting in the door of the naturalist's tent, watching a white-faced moon climb out of a ragged horizon of mountain crags.

"Never heard anything like it in my life! You say a party gave you those three beautiful black pearls because you agreed to let those pigs loose to run free in the jungle? Pigs you went all the way to Cochin China for? You say they owed their lives to the pigs? Well, damn me!"

The little American curio-hunter grinned cheerfully, lit a cigar, and blew a perfect succession of smoke rings.

"Listen," he announced. "I'll tell you the story."

Bradshaw stared in surprise. Peter Scarlet seldom related stories.

"Go on!" urged the naturalist, irritably.

"Ever see a Mohammedan eat ham?" asked the curio-hunter.

"Of course not! You know as well as I do that Mussulmans abhor pigs—"

"G'night, Brad," finished Scarlet abruptly. "That's the story."

Behind the Idol

Coming in an early issue is *The Idol Breaker*, another Peter Scarlet yarn by Roscoe. Not only does the author know that country, but his parents before him did. That Orient stuff just runs in his blood. Listen!

Eighteen-ninety-four and the *Chelidra* of the Indo-China Line was ploughing doggedly through the Straits of Malacca, heading for Singapore. One of the several passengers was my father; and the trip would have been far from entertaining, but for the efforts of the grizzled English skipper who stowed in his hold a great cargo of yarns. Sitting under the deck-awning, my father lent ear to the skipper unloading generous portions of his cargo, dishing up tales of Oriental adventure never to be forgotten.

"There was a yella-robed monk once—" and "Gold! Young fella, that their idol was solid!" On and on he went with the persistence of the waves drubbing the *Chelidra's* prow, the enthusiasm of the story-teller with a victim who appears to believe his tale. And then there was a stoker on a P. and O. boat out of Penang, a stoker whose tattooed chest was an education. And an old shrine somewhere in Siam—

The *Chelidra* may be gone. That skipper may be gone. But the yarns lived on with my father—my father, who has a son. His son is one of those chaps with a restless pen, an ink-spattered tie, an old hat, and the itch for phrases. Nineteen-twenty-seven and *The Idol Breaker.*

THEODORE ROSCOE

THE PHANTOM CASTLE
OF GENGHIZ KHAN

A yarn of Mongolia.

OLD DMITRIFF HAD been dying on his feet. That loathsome disease claiming more than one victim of Siberian prison exile for its own had laid foraging hands on the fugitive. Hourly his steps tottered the more; hourly his faltering increased. A ghastly wreck, that old Russian, smashed by an inhuman machine.

His face, shielded by kindly profusions of whisker, was crumbling away from the leprosy. Fever burned in his eyes. His back sagged, weighted by heavy chains welded to an iron collar clamped about his neck. His every move would rattle the fetters, and their gruesome clank, clink, clank as he wandered around camp sounded a dirge in Peter Scarlet's ear.

"Hellish noise," the curio-hunter complained to Montgomery, the young attaché of the British consular service at Samarkand, who was accompanying him to Kabul. "We ought to cut those chains from the poor devil's neck. That clanking will drive me mad."

Montgomery nodded, a dubious expression on his desert-tanned face. A startlingly handsome face, Montgomery's, burnt so brown that his blond hair looked white by comparison. He had a humorous mouth, and eyes steely as the bullets that had droned before them when chasing Germans off Lake Nyanza. He had a reckless spirit that had, after leaving Uganda, sent him joining *La Légion Etrangère*, service from which he had graduated with his only facial blemish, his left ear shot away by a Riff bullet. But for that scarred ear, Scarlet might not have recognized him in the amazing conclusion to this adventure.

"I don't think the Russian will live through the night," Montgomery answered Scarlet's comment. "He was most starved when we picked him up in the desert yesterday. The poor blighter dies to-night, or I miss my guess."

"Death should be a pleasure for him. Never saw such living misery in my life. How he journeyed across the steppes is a miracle to me."

"A chap'll do anything to jump one of those exiles," the young Briton returned. "Dmitriff says he and three others killed their guards, escaping together. A devilish time they had of it. Tsar's government used to pay Cossacks ten rubles a piece for every escaping jailbird. Dmitriff claims he's been wandering for ten years. His pals were all sniped off. Why, the chap hardly knows there's been a war. I say, he wanted to see you."

"Where is he now?"

"I bunked him in the caravan-master's tent," replied Montgomery. "Haroom was jolly peeved about it, but the beggar can put up with one of his cameleers. As I say, he can probably have his tent back before the night is done. Dmitriff won't eat anything. Just yabbles and groans, and guzzles your gin."

"Good. Let's take a look at him, again. Afraid of leprosy?"

"Hell, no. Ran into plenty in India, before they stationed me in this region."

Leaving Scarlet's tent, they strolled toward that of Haroom, the caravan-master.

Somber twilight was darkening the hushed desert lands. A spattering of early stars winkled faintly in vaulted sky. Dreary night clouds toiled along a barren ridge of hills that jutted on the rim of a broad, arid valley scooping away to the east. Quiet, almost evil, mantled the region. A forbidding region, promising relentless death to the unwary who would trap himself in its stern, waterless wastes, or fall prey to its Turkoman banditry, fierce, cruel as its heart.

Raising himself on his elbow, the dying
Russian panted out his story.

Scarlet remarked uneasily:

"Thank God only a few more days of this miserable caravaning, and we'll be in what little civilization Kabul has to offer. Lord knows I wouldn't have come out here but for those Turkoman rugs. But this damn country always hits me in the stomach."

"Sort of hell," agreed the other with a grin, waving his hand at the valley purpling in dusk. "Orient to the core, what? But I like it. Doesn't scare me half as much as your bloody old Malaya."

Past a somnolent group of moth-eaten camels, the great shuffle-footed beasts winking wicked eyes as they approached; past black tents in which Afghan cameleers busied themselves with noiseless tasks; past a morose, pink-bearded guard who saluted sullenly with one of those long rifles that shoot with incredible accuracy; they strolled to Haroom's tent. Scarlet lifted the flap; entered, followed by Montgomery.

On a mess of blankets the old Russian lay, a veritable heap of rags. He had been dozing, but on seeing visitors, his eyes from their black caverns, glimmered recognition. Withered hands trembled at his iron collar, and he spoke with effort.

"Ah; my friends. So good of you to come."

Scarlet extended a kindly hand.

"Sick?"

"Sick! *Bozhe moy!* I die." Words whispered from the formless mouth.

Montgomery lit a lantern. Wavering flame painted spectral shadows on the tent wall, cast a wan glow on the Russian's cadaverous face. The little American curio-hunter shivered, and Montgomery fumbled for his flask.

"Here," he offered. "Try a bracer, old chap."

"It is good. Very good. You have been kind, my friends, to a derelict and a burden. Now, I, on whom God's curse seems to have settled, shall repay you. Listen. Will you hear a story? The rum—thanks to you. Life in drying veins. Yes, a story. Not mine—that would be drab compared to this one. Draw closer. The Briton knows this land, do you not? Good. You have heard the legend of the phantom castle? The phantom castle of Genghiz Khan? Yes. Of course. For it is told from the frozen mountains of Thibet to the plateaus of Ust-Urt, from Kafiristan to the Kara Sea. But the little American with the bald head and white beard has not heard it. Listen."

Raising himself on his elbow, the dying Russian panted out his story. The story of Genghiz Khan, the Mongol Emperor, and his castle by the lost lake. A smart demon, the great Khan, and the Russian pictured him leading the mighty Tartar hordes that poured a conquering flame from their eastern hills. Pictured the whole, vast Central Asia suffering under the Mongol's bloody scimitar. Pictured the battles, the din, the cries of women, screams of men lusting blood, vile rags and mad riches, lurid hates and hells of that conquered empire. Piles of skulls bleached white, dotting the vanquished land; and piles of gems blazed in the courts of the great Genghiz.

One castle he built in a valley, so the story went, beside a crystal lake. He stuffed the castle with the most magnificent jewels of his realm, sapphires and rubies, red pearls big as plums, and emeralds as big as the buttons on a Cossack's cloak. And he stuffed the castle with two score beautiful, conquered women.

Those women moaned day and night, night and day, weeping for their lost men. They wept so hard their tears flooded the lake, and the lake, filling the valley basin, flooded the castle. Proof? Were not all lakes in that region salty? And ever after, at certain times favored by the moon, the vanished castle rises from its entombing waters; a bell tolls in the castle tower; and the castle sinks again into the mist—

Sweating with the effort, old Dmitriff gasped out the story: Scarlet and Montgomery listening like fools. They thought he was done when he sank back on his rags, but he flung himself up again with a fierce throb of energy that startled them. Words struck vehemence from his tongue.

"It's true! Hear me! Do you think I wandered alone, dragging my chains into this devil's land for nothing? Do you think I starved and baked and rotted for the pleasure? Not I? I did not! I came looking for those emeralds, those pearls! I hunted the phantom castle! And by the good God!" his claw-like hands knotted, his voice rattled. "I *found* it!"

With that verbal punch, he dropped back gurgling on the blankets. Peter Scarlet stared at Montgomery. The Englishman was mighty interested. He fell to his knees beside the twitching Russian; held high the lantern.

"Yes!" Dmitriff blew the word from his lungs. "I found the lost lake! Saw the phantom castle—heard the bell toll—heard it toll, I tell you! The Blessed Virgin knows I do not lie! And hearing the bell I was afraid—ran away—you found me—the lake lies—in the valley to the east, beneath the brown hills—the bell will toll—the castle will rise from the mists—full of emeralds—"

A sucked-in breath; a spasmodic wrench at the iron collar. The forced liquor, unswallowed, dribbled in the ragged beard. The coals of eyes burned away. Old Dmitriff had escaped.

Montgomery folded the hands on the wretched breast. Scarlet fumbled nervously with the lantern.

"All checks cashed," was the Englishman's laconic comment. "Poor beggar. He believed in his yarn. I say—"

He did not say. Instead, he stared like an image! Stood and stared! Scarlet listened, too, and listening, his blood pumped madly, his face flared astonishment.

Borne on the wings of a warm night wind off the desert came the faint, sonorous, sleepy clong of a tolling bell!

CLANG-CLONG. Clong-clang. Slow ringing echoed softly over the sands, desolate sands from which no bell should toll.

Peter Scarlet and his companion were not the only ones to hear the bell. Outside, a certain pink-bearded Afghan guard was drowsy no more. As the first solemn note clanged into the night, that guard hissed a Moslem oath of surprise, and fled for the tent where Haroom and his cameleers were enjoying a friendly hour of bickering. The guard burst in upon them. Words skipped fast in the tent. Rose a sudden cackle of curses, pungent prayers, then the icy tones of the caravan-master, cuffing them to silence.

Haroom's beady eyes sparkled, his leather-skinned face, weedy with black beard, reddened with rage.

"Be silent, sons of donkeys! There is no danger. You hear only a bell, the bell of Genghiz Khan. Quiet, Kadjr el-Ahmood, or I'll kick your ribs to little sticks! Be still! Are you women that an iron bell can terrify? Come, Ali Yar," he pointed at the guard, "saddle my pony! We shall go to find the bell, for once before in this region I heard it. Come, fool, the pony. Silence, mud-plastered idiots, or the vultures will feed on you to-morrow! Quick, Ali Yar, before the white swine find us gone, and wonder. By Allah's beard, I'll see where hides that bell!"

Stamping of pony hoofs, a whirl of gray burnoose, hoarse commands. Haroom and the Afghan guard were streaking across the desert in the darkness.

In the tent with the dead, Montgomery suddenly found voice.

"The lake, Scarlet! The lake in the valley! Hop a pony! We'll tear down there!"

The curio-hunter hesitated.

"The cameleers—"

"Dash 'em! If they heard it they're scared stiff. Listen, man! That's a real bell! If that castle and those emeralds are— Come on!"

Sprinting from the tent, they grabbed ponies, swung to saddle, and neck and neck, raced away in the night.

Pallid moon stole from behind gray cloud; rode lonely skies above the distant cliffs, its silvery light ghostly on the sands, casting deep shadows among the hills. Under looming banks of sandrock the riders fled, across arid washes, down treacherous dunes. Spirit of adventure stirred Scarlet's blood. Urging his mount to breakneck pace, he chased Montgomery's beast to desperate speed. The slopes fell away behind them. The hills outlined more clearly. The tolling bell sounded nearer.

An hour's gallop brought them into a tangle of shallow ravines which they followed to the base of the sand cliffs. Scarlet stared at the precipitous walls, shadowy in moonlight. Grim walls that had sat, thus, brooding the ages through: had frowned on the legions of vanished dynasties since the days of Eden; on the nomad empires of the Ouigurs; on the warring Tartar hordes of the mighty Genghiz; on the blood-spattered armies of Timur the Lame, Goondjur, and Amursan Khan: knew the epic mysteries that ten million years had bred on the breasts of Mother Asia. Peter Scarlet stared; felt puny; and was glad of the rifle at his saddle.

Following an ancient trail footing the cliffs, the riders gained an open plateau. There in the broad valley basin beneath them spread the salt lake, its crusted shore barren and dismal. Dismal, indeed. For rolling over the water billowed a thick, wet fog that brushed chilling fingers against Scarlet's face. The curio-hunter did not like that fog. Nor did Montgomery. It crawled so silently; would suddenly thin out, penetrated by moon ray, and reveal a patch of glittering black water. Somewhere from those misty depths the bell was tolling.

"Whew," snorted Scarlet. "I don't enjoy this! Can't see an inch into that stuff—thick as cotton!"

"The bell's out there, all right!" Montgomery exclaimed with an excited laugh. "If those damn clouds would only lift. Come on, Scarlet. Let's get to the beach."

They scrambled down a steep incline to the shore. Scarlet stared helplessly at the fog-hung water; shivered in the dampness. Montgomery cursed impatiently.

"Can't see a thing! What do you say to— But look!"

Like swirling white smoke the fog bank rolled away, suddenly unveiling a sight so strange as to make Scarlet yell, and Montgomery squawk in amazement. Three hundred feet from shore an ancient castle tower thrust green, moss-covered walls from the churning waves. Trailing mists lingered about the spired turret which glistened in the moonlight. Crumbling, weedy windows showed gloomy holes in the tower wall. At the waterline a porchlike balcony over which water foamed led to an arched doorway. High in the turret a rusty bell swung, slowly in the wind, tolling its somnolent clong. A mighty weird sight. A specter from centuries long dead. The phantom castle. They dismounted and hobbled their ponies.

"Wow!" gasped the curio-hunter. "Look at that! By God, it wasn't there when we passed along the trail this morning! The castle! Monty! What the hell are you doing?"

The Englishman had ripped off his jacket; was kicking loose his boots.

"Coming?" he cried. "Emeralds, the old Russian said. Man! I'm going to swim out there!"

An uninviting invitation.

"Wait!"

"Wait, hell!"

Naked and like a bronze statue he stood on the shore, waiting while Scarlet tore off his clothing. Moonlit water revealed a sheer bank of rock dropping deep at their feet. Together they plunged into the lake.

If Montgomery was a good swimmer so was Scarlet, and the little curio-hunter stroked through the icy water with a steady

Trailing mists lingered
about the spired turret which
glistened in the moonlight.

motion that brought him to the tower at the Englishman's side. Lurking in the clear depths beneath them glimmered mossy, sunken castle walls. Montgomery drew himself up on the balcony; helped Scarlet up. Trembling with cold, they peered into the castle's black interior. Then voicing a sharp oath, the young Englishman stepped inside. Scarlet followed.

A dreary quiet, broken by the drip-dripping of water and the muffled tolling of the bell above, breathed sepulchral atmosphere from the dank tower. Odor of rotting weeds clung about the musty walls. The tower's base was submerged, but a circular stone stairway climbed to an inner balcony that loomed in the murky darkness over their heads. Murky darkness dispelled by moonbeams straying through one of the windows high in the turret. Wind rose, and the bell tolled louder. Peter Scarlet experienced an acute desire to be elsewhere.

Not so Montgomery. That young Englishman was verily in his Seventh Heaven. He chuckled with delight; motioned Scarlet to follow, and started crawling up the winding stair. Half-fearing every move would plunge him into the black water below, Scarlet crawled after. Those steps were hell. They were just that. For the stones were decaying, loose, and slippery with oozey slime. Montgomery laughed.

"Pretty solid stuff for a ghost castle."

And his voice echoed hollowly in the gloom "—for a ghost castle."

The balcony achieved, they slid carefully over clammy flag-stones; brought to a halt on their knees before a massive door, glassy as marble, bolted by an iron bar—now a mere thread of rust. Straining his eyes in the darkness, Scarlet discerned the door as wrought over with the scrawling marks of an old in-scription. Knocking the rusted bolt away with a blow from his fist, Montgomery put shoulder to stone and shoved. The door was wedged fast, but pushing with every ounce of power, Mont-gomery finally moved it, and it swung in with a senile groan. Mouldy breath redolent of buried years rushed out with the dead wind. The yells of Montgomery and Peter Scarlet were simultaneous!

Echo answered from the turret gloom "—My God!"

That moonlight straying from the turret window slanted into a vault-like room—a chamber closed centuries before by the hands of some terrified servant of the Khans and since that time had remained unopened.

Moonbeams falling through the open door were scattered about the room and were snatched up, caught, and tossed back, glinting and glistening and winking, a thousand dancing rays. Rays that sparkled on Peter Scarlet's broad brow, sifted in his snowy beard; shimmered in the Englishman's astounded eyes.

No water had ever penetrated that sealed vault. No corrod-ing waves had ever dimmed the glory of that ancient chamber's treasure. Red pearls, big as plums, the Russian had said; sapphires and rubies, emeralds big as the buttons on a Cossack's cloak.

The legend had not lied about the castle, and it did not lie about those gems. They blazed, glimmered, and sparkled moonbeams like ten thousand little stars heaped on the vault floor, piled in brass bowls, spilling from age-rotted boxes.

Scarlet was sick, sick with wonder. He stared, and his companion stared, mouth agape. Clong-clang came the muffled tolling of the tower bell. Water dripped rhythmically. Colored lights scintillated on mossy, green walls.

Montgomery broke the quiet with a shrill oath. Scarlet flung around. Sounded a faint splashing without.

And then in the arched tower entrance stood two naked men. In the fist of one, whose pink beard dribbled water, glinted a vicious *yataghan*, a sickle-like Tartar scimitar. In the fist of the other, whose weedy beard showered drops as he wagged his little, skull-like head, gleamed a nasty, crooked dagger. Clong-clang rang the somber knell from above.

"HAROOM!"

"By Allah! We saw you from the shore—"

With a flash of steel, Montgomery struck. His yell crashed in the shadows, as he flung himself down the steps, whipped beating fists to the Turkoman's face. Scarlet barely dodged the hurled dagger, skidded down the stairway, ducked a beheading swipe from the Afghan's scimitar, and clamped hands on the brown throat beneath the pink beard. On perilous footing of slimy stone they battled; Haroom's grunts sounding with the smack of the Englishman's fists; Ali Yar's wheezy, whistling gasps mingling with Scarlet's cursing as the Afghan's fingers clawed across his face.

Down went Montgomery and Haroom, the later fighting to reach Ali Yar's fallen scimitar. Down went the Afghan and Scarlet, Ali gouging a finger into the curio-hunter's cheek, but fortunately missing the eyes which had been his objective.

With a flash of steel,
Montgomery struck.

Scarlet lost his choking grip, and, locked in his enemy's arms,
splashed into the black water beneath the inner balcony. Under
they sank, the curio-hunter fighting in mad frenzy at the arms
dragging him down; drowning him. With a final frantic kick
he wrenched free, drove a deadly punch at the naked, clinging
body, and shot to the surface. From the murky depths a stream
of bubbles followed. Treading water, Scarlet cleared his eyes,
and saw a grim struggle writhing on the balcony stair.

Squirming in the grip of a strangle-hold, Haroom had
managed to fasten teeth in Montgomery's wrist. Groaning, the
young Englishman was striving to twist the Turkoman's head.

Fighting for their lives, they were. For their lives, and the gems that played dancing lights on the green walls above them.

Scarlet drew himself to the landing, and started up the slippery steps. Started up the steps, and found water rising to his knees. Terrified, he turned to see the archway, which had been above water level, immersed to half its height. Swirling waves were foaming into the tower, rippling over the stones. The curio-hunter screamed.

"We're sinking! Montgomery! Quick! For the love of God!"

The Englishman's laugh rang brittle above a soprano shriek from Haroom. Bone snapped with a sickening crack. The body of the caravan-master flopped down the steps, to sink in a frothy tumble of water. Swaying drunkenly on the top step, Montgomery laughed again.

Came a lurch that split a gaping crack in the tower wall. The castle trembled in the grip of a subterranean spasm. A gush of water nearly swept Scarlet from his feet. With a cry, he battled to gain the fast-filling archway.

"Quick! Montgomery!"

No answer.

The curio-hunter flung around; saw the young Englishman turn and scramble for the open door of the treasure-chamber; saw him disappear through the entrance. And then Peter Scarlet screeched in dismay. A tremor jostled the castle walls, jarred a mighty clong from the tower bell. And the stone door of the vault swung shut with a tremendous slam; Montgomery's cry stifled in the closed room. Water poured into the tower. Scarlet dove, fought his way under the arch, ducked under the flooded coping, and bobbed up outside of those sinking walls.

The moon was creeping behind clouds driven by moaning winds. Waves were churning over the lake's troubled surface. With all his strength, with cold, mad fury Peter Scarlet battled them to shore; where, naked, sobbing, alone, he stood on the desolate beach. The little American curio-hunter stood, and watched foaming waters close over the tower walls, the bell swinging in the turret, tolling its sullen curfew to the last, its somber clong echoing mournfully among the hills.

PETER SCARLET knocked the ashes from his cigar, and stared across the bungalow verandah, cross the tranquil, purple-shadowed bay at feathery clouds tracing an old-lace pattern against tinted sunset sky. He had been briefly telling a story, and sweat glistened on his forehead. His companion thought he looked very old.

"Well," he related after hesitant pause, "I finally got to Kabul. In a crazy state of mind, you can bet. I surely was. But in Kabul I ran into a Russian Engineer, a scientist; old friend of mine I once met back in th' days of the Russo-Japanese War. Told Seminovitch the story I just told you. And he said all that damn country was liable to strange eruption; earth tremors at certain times of year. Said the tides in some of those lakes, especially farther north, are astonishing. The lake beds subject to sudden elevations or depressions, if you get the idea. And that castle's appearance was due to some, well, what he called tectonic geological disturbance, or something."

Scarlet sighed; turned to his waiting *stenger* of whiskey and soda. He seemed expecting comment.

Holmes Bradshaw, the gaunt American naturalist, grunted sceptically.

"A thumping good yarn, Peter. A wonderful story, or a whopper!"

The curio-hunter made an impatient gesture.

"I told you at the start you wouldn't believe it. But hell that's not the half of it! Not half! Say! From Kabul I went into India; from there over to Aden where I stayed a couple of months to ease up nerves in the dullest place I know. Coming back to Malaya—now get this—the boat put up at Bombay. Now don't ask questions. Questions, hell—" Scarlet spat vehemently. "The Orient is no place for questions. Well, I was rushing down th' Appolo Bunder dock in a hell of a hurry when I ran smack into some fool sprinting for a boat. Dumped me over, and knocked my hat over my eyes. And I cursed plenty, you can bet. And I heard a laugh! A loud laugh! 'Scarlet!' cries a voice. 'Peter Scarlet! You're in luck!' Pulled off my hat, and saw a chap standing fumbling in his pocket, grinning like a fool. Wow! I nearly died, I tell you! That fellow laughed out loud. His face was battered for fair, and he looked skinny as a rail, but prosperous as hell. Lord! 'I got out!' he yells. 'Here, take this! Souvenir! Gotta catch boat. See you again, old blighter! Take it! Got a bucket full!' And pressing something into my hand, away he dashes. Oh, it was him, all right. Montgomery! Might not o' known th' damned idiot but for his left ear gone. It was him. And he got out. You bet he had. Him and his bucket full. That young devil could have got out of hell—"

Digging fiercely in his pocket, Scarlet drew out a small leather bag; untied the strings. Into his brown palm rolled a single green fire, a matchless emerald that glimmered at Bradshaw through twilight dusk. Glimmered and winked and twinkled, sprinkling points of fire into shadowy corners of the verandah. A matchless emerald, big as the button on Cossack's cloak.

> *It is a well-known fact that due to a number of causes, some well known, others as yet not so well understood, a number of lakes in Siberia and Mongolia are known to change their level from time to time. It is said in one case on good authority that a lake moves constantly. In fifty years the lake has moved nearly forty miles and has completely submerged several villages. Currents and tides are likewise produced by high winds and shallow bays. In Africa the level and outlet of lakes have been much altered by volcanic action. Lakes Tanganyika and Kivu were a part of the Nile sources, but now, because of the comparatively recent dam of Volcanoes, they form a portion of the Congo system. So in the beds of certain Siberian and Mongolian lakes there is a little known volcanic action which from time to time throws up islands which just as suddenly vanish. Many legends hinge on these little known phenomena, among them the above. Marquard, Osandowski and others have written of these phenomena, also J.E.S. Moore and Sir Harry Johnston.*

BLOOD RITUAL

*Weird chants warned him away, yet Peter
Scarlet craved the mysterious battle-axe—
to find it all too close to his throat!*

PETER SCARLET SPAT impatiently through his beard.

"Then you won't go back there with me?"

The Malay boy shook his head.

"No, *tuan*. Evil spirits haunt the place. From the mission bungalow came strange chanting and much awful music. I was afraid."

"He was only playing hymns on his organ," snapped Scarlet. "I can't see why you were afraid to go near. He was singing."

"Perhaps, *tuan*. But the song was strange to the ear. And I planted two little white flags in the path to guard me from spirits, and I called to the white man telling him of your journey here."

"Yes, and then he told you to tell me I can call on him if I *dare*," puzzled the curio-hunter. "Mighty queer thing for him to say, I'll admit. He's always glad when I visit him. You say he didn't come out of the bungalow? Didn't he bid you any greeting?"

"He did not, *tuan*. The chanting started again, and I ran away, for the voice was very low and whispery and strange. It made me think of the evil spirits that travel jungle rivers at night. The place is beset with evil, *tuan*. In my returning path lay a great python coiled in a black pool. A bad sign."

Scarlet set aside the swizzle stick with which he had been mixing his virgin (vermouth and gin); paused; gulped down the drink.

"Ismail, I can't believe an educated chap like you is a super-stitious fool. Damned funny business, this. I send you off on an errand to the mission, and you come back with a wild-eyed yarn about evil charms and mysterious music. I'm going to get to the bottom of it. If you won't go up there, I'll go alone! Why, boy, the *padre tuan* is meek as Moses; wouldn't hurt a flea."

"He would not, *tuan*. But I was not sure the missionary was there. The voice was not exactly his. You call me superstitious. No. There are some things a native can sense. The white man must see. A native can feel. I felt the spirit of evil. It is foolish to go there," the Malay insisted.

The curio-hunter tapped his boot in irritation.

"If something is wrong, then I want to find it out. You fellows are too woozy for anything. I'm going up and see Ashley, anyway. If it wasn't his voice, it was a visitor or somebody. I know you Malays have a nose for smelling evil, but I'm not going to let such nonsense scare me off. I came up here to call on the *padre tuan,* and I'm going to see him. Pack that kit of mine. Get the 22-bore rifle. Stick in some aspirin. I'm going up the river."

Ismail shrugged and hurried to provision the curio-hunter's kit. Alone, Scarlet mixed another virgin. Staring moodily into the gloomy jungle that swarmed about his bungalow, he complained to himself:

"Can't do a blessed thing in this country without running into a lot of hoodoo-voodoo of some kind. Nonsense. Wonder what really did scare Ismail away? These Malays aren't so dumb. Something may be wrong with Ashley or the mission. That python couldn't have scared him away. This dump just crawls with 'em."

Waiting for his boy to return, he lit a cigar and puffed uneasily. Suddenly brilliant afternoon sunlight was blotted out, wind whipped through the bamboo grove. In half a second pouring rain was sluicing the clearing. As abruptly the sun shone bright again. When the curio-hunter stepped from the verandah the stream before his bungalow was boiling like a river, the steaming jungle dripped water and was alive with leeches.

"Fool country! Drenched one second, burnt crisp the next," was his sour comment, as he shouldered into his pack. "I'll be back in camp tomorrow night. If Bradshaw *tuan* comes from Kelantan while I'm away, make him comfortable. That means mix him some drinks. Tell him I've gone to the mission, and to wait for me. Have some food ready," was his parting command.

But Peter Scarlet did not return the next night. Nor the next. Bradshaw, the visiting naturalist from Kelantan, grew impatient, worried, and drank a great many *stengers* of whisky and soda.

And Ismail, the Malay boy, set out little white flags to propiti-
ate the evil spirits.

SOFT, scented Asian night hung her thick veils over the jungle
land, and pinned them with a crescent moon. With the coming
darkness, a low disharmony of bird-calls rose from the creeper-
woven undergrowth. Swallows twittered. A hornbill called its
weird "whoo-whoo-ha-ha-ha!" Legions of frogs chorused in
the river swamp. Bats streaked in crazy flight over the black
water.

Peter Scarlet drew his shallow craft up on the mud bank,
slung his rifle under his arm, to strike off through the thickets
of clumpy bamboo. About him the jungle rustled with busy life.
Soon the darkness was filled with a perfect medley of toots,
coughs, squawks and screeches. Though he was used to these
night sounds, the curio-hunter was glad when his path led into
a clearing, and through the trees he saw yellow patches of light
gleaming from the mission bungalow. Striding to the dark
verandah, he let his pack slip from his shoulders.

"Halloo!" he called.

Matting was pushed aside. A large figure stood outlined in
the doorway, lamplight gleaming faintly on long white locks
tumbling over the great shoulders, on the flowing beard snowy
as Scarlet's own, and on the white *sarong* that fell to the wear-
er's sandals.

"Tabay, tuan," came the sonorous greeting in Malay; and in
a swish of white the giant missionary stepped to the verandah.
Light fell from the open door; revealed the curio-hunter with
outstretched hand. Seeing his visitor in better light, the missionary hurried forward.

"Peter Scarlet! Well, well. Had no idea you were in the region.
Thought it was one of the natives stopping by. Come right in,
my friend. It is good to see a white face. Very good. You know
how lonely a man gets here sometimes."

If Scarlet had owned to any previous uneasiness, his fears were allayed. They shook hands warmly, and the curio-hunter said familiarly:

"Mighty glad to see you, Ashley. Been nearly two years since the last time. You're looking fit. Marvelous to me how you keep the fever out of your bones. How goes the Anglican Church these days? And how's the mission?"

"God's work always demands patience," replied the old man, leading Scarlet into the bungalow. "As to the church, I cannot say. But here all is work, work, work. But now—" taking Scarlet's kit and rifle—"sit down, Peter. Let me bring you some tea. I'll have to make it myself—the boys are away. We can chat better with moistened tongues. No doubt you'd prefer a *stenger,*" he added with a smile, "but I preach strict temperance to my little flock and, therefore, exact it of myself. If you greatly desire one, I can possibly get some about."

"Not at all, *padre.* I haven't forgotten the way you brew tea. First tell me—did not my Malay boy make known my coming?"

The missionary shook his shaggy head thoughtfully.

"Nobody has been here in the last few days, Peter. I have been quite alone of late. I did not see your boy."

"Damned bit of nonsense," Scarlet muttered to himself, as the missionary quitted the room. "I can't imagine what threw such a fuss into Ismail. Why in hell did he cook up that evil-spirit yarn?"

With a shrug, Scarlet seated himself on one of the several benches in the room. After pulling three fat leeches from his arm, he idly gazed about him. The mission presented a familiar appearance. In one corner stood a small organ littered with hymnals. Near the organ leaned a rickety table on which lay a huge Bible with a brass clasp. A plain wooden cross hung on the wall back of the table. And in strange contrast on the opposite wall hung an ancient *bliong,* a tremendous battle-axe of wrought steel.

That battle-mace was one of the reasons Scarlet called on Ashley's mission. The curio-hunter would have given his soul to own it. For years it had rusted on that wall, and a quaint, villainous weapon it was. To date he had never been able to induce the missionary to part with it. He was examining it with delight when the *padre* returned bearing porcelain bowls of tea.

"Always revives me after a hard day's work," the old missionary admitted, quaffing the brew with gusto. "Yes. And I've been working very hard. It has been very hot. At times my head sings with quinine."

"You've done a great work among the natives," was Scarlet's comment. "You ought to knock off, and take a run back to England, *padre*."

"I've worked hard in the heat," the missionary went on. "Studying scripture. Reading old texts. Preaching. Hard, hot work." He passed a tired hand across his face. "Peter, let me tell you something," he announced in a low voice.

Scarlet looked up in surprise; set his tea bowl in his lap.

"What is it, *padre*?"

"The will of the Almighty be done," whispered the old missionary sternly. And, with the words, out shot a malletlike fist that crashed squarely on the curio-hunter's jaw. Scarlet whirled over backward, tea flying over his jacket, the bowl smashing on the floor and scattering porcelain in his beard.

The *padre* chuckled; stroked his silky beard; stared dreamily at the figure crumpled on the floor. Then hastily drawing a stool before his little organ, he sent knotty fingers wandering over the keys. Mellow, majestic cadence of a hymn pealed from beneath his touch. Deep from his throat came a rhythmic chant that was low, and whispery, and strange.

THE LITTLE American curio-hunter had undergone more than one harrowing experience during his wanderings over the Orient. Age alone had not silvered his beard and stolen the hair from his crown. He was no novice at facing the grim scythe-wielder or the grimmer grip of the torturer. But his two nerve-tweaking days in the captivity of that mad Anglican missionary surely etched crow's-feet about his eyes and tinted his beard the whiter.

There was something peculiarly horrible in the mad *padre's* insanity. He would have flashes of mental balance that would give the little curio-hunter, lying bound and gagged in a back room, momentary hope. He would place a cool hand on his captive's forehead and stare compassionately at the pale face.

"And why have they imprisoned you, my poor man?"

And the next second he would mumble most savage oaths, the more shocking as they came from behind so benevolent an expression.

Visitors called several times. Even as he had deceived Scarlet, the madman chatted calmly with them, asked them in. Scarlet could hear the gentle voice quoting Scripture. Perhaps the callers, with canny native intuition, detected an alien note in the missionary's tone as Ismail had done, for the second day no visitors came.

All through the stifling mid-day heat the missionary played his organ. Play, play, play! The little instrument wheezed with hymn after hymn. And Peter Scarlet sweated in an agony of apprehension.

"He's raving mad," was all Scarlet could think, when interspersed with a stately chant would come a solemnly muttered oath. "He's a maniac. Heat and quinine have done for him. No telling how long he's been off. Or what in heaven's name he'll try and do with me—"

What would the madman do? The thought tortured Scarlet more than thirst, heat, and the suffocating gag in his teeth. And with increasing fear, Scarlet fought at his bonds. He wrenched. He kicked. He rolled over the floor, writhed, squirmed and wrestled. But he could not loosen the thongs strapping wrists and ankles. He could not loosen them one particle. Panting, with bleeding wrists and sinking heart, he was forced to lie quietly in the dark.

That first night was interminable. The curio-hunter ached with the suspense of it. When he had come to consciousness, found himself bound, and realized what had happened, he had struggled against sleep. Before morning he had prayed for it. All night long the madman had chanted and mumbled out of the darkness. And Scarlet had wished a scorpion might bite him and terminate the strain.

Exhaustion overcame the captive the following day. And the second night Peter Scarlet slept as best a man can with a dirty rag over his mouth, a throat screaming thirst, and limbs groaning with cramps.

At dawn he was awakened by the missionary, who stood like a patriarch from Old Testament days, mysterious in the gray light, smiling sadly on the sodden figure at his feet. Scarlet read blankness in the eyes beneath the silvery locks, and shivered.

The mad *padre* sighed. Reaching down, he lifted the curio-hunter in his arms, carried him with amazing ease from the bungalow, down a weaving jungle trail, across a treacherous swamp, to a mossy glade deep in a palm grove. At one end of the glade stood a crude stone altar. The unhappy captive was stretched out on this altar and, despite his feeble struggles, was bound down with hemp the madman carried in his *sarong*.

No pleasing situation for the little curio-hunter. Face up, he stared at the scattered puffs of cloud sailing in the azure morning sky; stared at the sky and wondered if God was taking a day off; stared at the sky through leafy fronds of a palm that drooped above the altar, and wondered if he would ever see that sky again. His numbed brain strove with fleeting ideas. He hardly realized his captor had slipped away in the jungle, been gone for half an hour. But he realized it when the missionary returned.

For the missionary returned chanting a hymn; and under his right arm he bore the huge Bible with the brass clasp, and under his left arm he carried the *bliong*, that tremendous Malay battle-axe wrought of steel!

The missionary did not hesitate with his program. He placed the Bible at Scarlet's feet, and leaned the mace against the altar. Then, stretching both hands over the bound man, he crooned a jargon of garbled ritual. A strange scene! Yellow sunlight slanting into the cool glade, sunbeams straying in the shaggy silvery hair of the madman, sparkling on the brass clasp of the Bible, glinting on the steel mace, glistening on Peter Scarlet's sweat-bathed face.

His ritual done, the madman picked up the Bible. Holding it close to his eyes, he read aloud in funereal tones:

" 'And it came to pass after these things, that God did tempt Abraham, and said unto him, Abraham: and he said, Behold, here I am. And he said, Take now thy son, thine only son Isaac whom thou lovest, and get thee into the land of Moriah: and offer him there for a burnt offering.… And Abraham rose up early in the morning, and saddled his ass, and took two of his young men and Isaac his son, and clave the wood for the burnt offering, and rose up and went into the place of which God had told him.… And Abraham took the wood of the burnt offering, and laid it upon Isaac, his son; and he took the fire in his hand and a knife, and they went both of them together.… And they came to the place which God had told him of: and Abraham built an altar there, and laid the wood in order, and bound Isaac his son, and laid him on the altar on the wood. And Abraham stretched forth his hand, and took the knife to slay his son—' "

Whereupon the mad missionary slammed shut the Book, and snatched up the battle-axe.

Fighting in frenzy, Scarlet had managed to work the gag loose. With a fierce effort he spat the cloth from his mouth, and cried out, his voice thick and dry:

"Ashley! Stop! Wait! Ashley! Ashley!"

"Ashley?" murmured the madman. "What means that?"

Poising the axe above Scarlet's throat, he stared soberly at the curio-hunter.

"My God!" squawked Scarlet. "Don't murder me! Wait!"

"Heard you not the Scriptures?"

Peter Scarlet never knew how he came to remember it at that desperate hour—it had been years since he had heard the story.

"Stop!" he screamed. "Stop! You didn't finish the passage. God called from heaven and told Abraham not to sacrifice Isaac. The old fool sacrificed a ram instead." He sobbed.

"So he did," returned the missionary gravely. "And long have I waited to hear the Lord's voice. If he calls to me now, I shall know he is in heaven, and you shall go free. I shall stay my hand a moment. Let the Almighty speak!"

Followed an awful minute of silence—a bad moment for the little American curio-hunter, a ghastly moment, with the madman's axe waiting to fall on the unprotected throat. Wind stirred the palms, rustled the missionary's white *sarong*. Poisonous, hot stench crept from nearby swamps. Quiet of the grave wrapped a sombre cloak about the jungle. A horrible moment. Peter Scarlet closed his eyes.

"I am waiting," whispered the missionary, "to hear the voice from heaven."

And he heard it!

From the tangled verdure above Scarlet's head came a muffled cow-like grunting. A sinuous, swaying neck curved down from the thatch of green. Scarlet's yell echoed with the missionary's gurgling cry, as a great python dropped its coiling body over the curio-hunter.

The shock of the serpent's fall knocked the last spark of consciousness from Scarlet's wracked frame. He did not hear the missionary's dreadful scream; did not see the battle-axe flash in the sunlight. Swung in frantic hands, the *bliong* swept down like a bolt of white lightning, snipped off that python's head clean as a razor slash, and just shaved a thin slice from the curio-hunter's shoulder. The headless serpent slipped lashing to the ground. Blood gushed about the stone altar.

White as summer cloud went the missionary's face. With trembling hands he wiped his eyes, stared at the squirming reptile at his feet; stared in amazement at the unconscious man bound to the altar. A tremor shook him. His cry rang among the trees.

"Peter Scarlet! In God's name! That snake! How—Scarlet! Peter! It is I—Ashley! The *padre!*"

BRADSHAW, the naturalist from Kelantan, was astounded at his friend's appearance. And Peter Scarlet surely made a strange picture, limping into camp on the arm of the aged *padre* from upstream. The curio-hunter's face was sun-scorched berry red, his wrists bandaged, his shoulder bound up, his teeth chattering with the fever. He was in a vile temper; would not answer a single question, and drank up virgins with a steady, dogged industry that soon put him to sleep.

The old missionary could explain nothing. Apparently he did not know what had occurred.

"Bradshaw," he confided to the naturalist, "it is all very strange. Peter talks so queerly. I haven't the slightest idea what happened to him. I haven't been so well myself. Been staying close to the mission, doctoring up with quinine. Found Peter in the jungle. He won't tell how he got there. Most peculiar. Between you and me, I think the heat or something may have deranged his mind for a time."

The naturalist was not so sure the *padre* was wrong. He told the curio-hunter what Ashley had said; and Scarlet laughed an ironical laugh—a strange laugh, a laugh that was very strange, indeed!

And hearing it, Ismail, the Malay boy, nodded sagely and planted a score of little white flags to ward off the evil spirits that travel up jungle rivers at night.

Blood Talk

By all means, hombre, read *Blood Ritual,* another of those Peter Scarlet yarns by Theodore Roscoe, in this issue. The weltering torrid heat of the Chino seas and Malay jungles are second nature to him; he doesn't make up stories—he just relates tales of the everyday life he has known down there.

Furnace sky, blistering sun, mercury lingering around the hundred and twenty mark. Heat ninety-five in the "cool" bungalow at night. In such a swelter as this my mother lived for years and, incidentally, enjoyed it. Born to it. But no wonder some of the sweating members of the white colony in Bareilly, who had experienced to date nothing hotter, perhaps, than a London music hall, grew depressed and even succumbed to temporary madness.

Such was the case with one of my mother's friends. Rising temperature and an overdose of quinine snapped the roof right off his head. Away he went tearing across the compound raving crazy, flailing his arms, reciting poetry, prayer and profanity. And little surprise—since he had downed almost six times the prescribed amount of quinine. When finally captured and subdued, he hardly realized what had happened.

From that incident, well recalled by my mother whose many years in the Orient are green to memory, I conceived the idea for the yarn. Mixed in with Malay (old stamping ground of my father's) setting, the little American curio-hunter playing the lead—and *Blood Ritual* seemed to write itself.

THEODORE ROSCOE

CLAWS OF THE NIGHT

Scarlet, Yankee dare-devil on off-trails, gambles
for treasure against the eerie might of the Orient.

IBRAHIM DREW THE knife from his sash, and looked inquiringly at his companion.

The other shook his head. His piggy eyes squinted to black buttons; chubby lips pursed in scornful smile.

"Not that, fool! The white dogs—Allah curse their bones—would catch and tie us up by our necks. Saw you not your friend, Achmed, legs kicking and face purple, thus, on the end of a string! Murder is pleasant, but dangerous. Theft is easy risk. These English hunt years for the killer, but by very commonness of number are forced to forget the thief. So Achmed was a fool. And you are a fool. A knife—pah! The way of the beggar who crawls in the lane!"

"What way do you advise, then, fat fish who knows all?"

"Patience, mud-heap, and listen to words of wisdom. Lend ear to Fazululla, and grow wise."

The bulky Arab rose to snatch aside the tent flap. Pointing with a pudgy finger, he said:

"See. There lies the treasure cave, across that narrow neck of beach. Do you think a man could pass over that strip of sand without being seen? As well hide in a red shirt! Stupid as they are, the Englishmen would see you and drive little lead balls into your head before you could cry Allah! How else can you approach the cave? The sea lies beside it; sheer rock above. That is the only path. By the Beard of the Prophet, it would take the devil himself to gain that cave alive!"

Ibrahim grunted, and spat. "Perhaps that is so. How, then, do you propose to lay hand on the jewels?"

Fazululla sighed sadly, as if profoundly miserable at his friend's low mentality, and returned to squat beside his *hookah*. For several moments he puffed in silence. The water bubbled gently in the jar. Fingers of smoke curled about his yellow turban.

"I have a plan," he wheezed finally. "And by Allah's blessing, it shall work well. Why should you know it? Suffice that a portion of the reward goes to you. Now answer this. When does the little white lizard called Scarlet leave for the town?"

"Tonight he departs, intent on traveling the dark hours through so that he may return by noon two days hence. I go with him. You stay with the camel-drivers."

"So. Tell me more. This Englishman—this long-faced swine who is to stay and guard the jewels—is he not the white engineer who is known for the strange music of his wooden box with strings?"

"The same."

"And is he not famed for his purity of heart; certain silly integrities? A man who will have naught of women?"

"He, and no other. As I told you, his name is known across the desert. The jades in Port Said halls dance like *houris* to attract him, but he spurns them all."

"Well told, little slug. Go you with the bearded, bald donkey to the town. And when you return the treasure will be gone. And so will I. You can meet me at the hidden shrine in Beersheba. The treasure and I will be gone. As so will this staunch Englishman of so honest heart, who is left to guard. He, also, will be gone!"

"**THAT** fat Arab has the eyes of a mongoose!" Peter Scarlet confided to Cameron. "And the grin of a snake. I feel uneasy every second he's out of my sight. I didn't get a smart look at him the night I hired him for a guide. No I didn't. His outfit was good, and he didn't haggle the price from one end of hoopoo to the other. But daylight brings him out with the face of a crook, the Allah yowling thief!"

The little American curio-hunter exhaled a fog of staggering smoke that enveloped the peak of the tent, and petulantly flung away his cigar. Wayne Cameron grinned.

"I won't trust him an inch, Peter. Leave it to me. You can tell the Arabs that the first man-jack to set foot on the beach in front of this cave will get his face shot off! I'm not anxious to get a knife in the neck. But don't worry. You've been out here a week, now, and the country has got your goat."

"It has, Cameron. I always did own a set of nerves. Sometimes the East twangs them like all get-out, and this place more than ever. Damned hole just stifles a man!"

He waved a hand at the landscape spreading before their tent—a picture, lifeless and forbidding, of sullen wastes scarred by legions of arid limestone cliffs that clutched ragged fingers at the iron sky. Wasteland bowed under the gray mantle of desolation peculiar to all volcanic regions. At the foot of stern cliffs washed salty watery of the Dead Sea. The shore was ruthlessly naked, sterile gray lava beds, jagged juts of vitreous rock. A dreary, barren land, this southern basin of the Dead Sea. A deadly region, shunned by man. El Ghor, the Arabs call it, "The Trough," a trough in which pours terrific heats, blinding sandstorms, bitter thirsts. Handiwork of nature in her most vicious mood.

Scarlet snorted uneasily. "No place for a Christian, much less a Yankee. Dead Sea is right. Dead. And buried. Only live things in this country are the fleas and that bird Fazululla. I'll be right glad to get out of here. Thank God, Cameron, that you came along! I wouldn't trust another man living with that treasure the way I trust you. You won't leave vigil for a second, will you boy?"

"Of course I won't!"

"Good. It's foolish of me to insist so much. I'm excited I guess. Lord, what a priceless collection there is! Those old gems probably been there since the days of David. War spoils! Battles fought by the tribesmen of Judah! I tell you, Cameron, when I bought those parchment scrolls off that crazy old Samaratine, I thought I was stung for fair. But when deciphering proved them genuine, and I came out here and found the treasure-vault just as indicated by the old records, I could have died! Let me tell you, it's a great find! Whew! Worth a young fortune! Worst of it was when I realized I couldn't touch it without sanction of the authorities. Didn't know what to do. Didn't dare leave it, now I'd opened the stone vault door and couldn't seal it again. And I didn't dare remove it, you know, until I pulled wool with the high hinky-dinks for permission. Then you happen by. Lord, what pure luck! No one else I'd rather leave it with, you can bet that!"

The young engineer voiced an embarrassed laugh. "I'll see you through, Peter. But get back as soon as you can, won't you? I'm aching for the sight of a hotel-cooked meal, and my old violin. Sometimes I get sick, yearning for that instrument, lonesome nights on the desert when I'm abandoned to a gang of sullen Arabs and molting camels."

"I won't be long. I knew you'd stay. I'll take your *dragoman*, Ibrahim, along with me. You say he knows the trail in. And we can get back in two days at the latest."

Scarlet buckled on his automatic, and reached for his helmet.

"You can hold out against a regiment with your position here," was his final advice. "Just stick in your tent, and keep a weather eye out all the time. I'm depending on you."

Their firm clasps met.

"I appreciate your trust, Peter," said the young engineer. "Nothing in the world will budge me from my post."

"Fine! Don't hesitate to shoot if trouble starts snooping around—in the robes of an Arab guide, for instance. Wager a million that fat Arab is sweating his beard off wondering what I'm hunting and finding out here. Men don't come into this hell-hole for nothing. No sir. Fazululla is wise!"

As he hurried down the beach toward the camp where Ibrahim waited with the horses, Peter Scarlet murmured to himself:

"He's the one man I can trust, Wayne Cameron is! Honest as Gibraltar. He'll stand guard, despite that wise-faced Arab sneak."

The curio-hunter had guessed Fazululla was wise, but would have been far more uneasy had he known just *how* wise that Arab was.

WAYNE CAMERON'S was not the soul of an engineer. He had slipped into the profession as logical conclusion of money-less campaigning with Allenby, at the close of the war. Nor had he ever been meant for the Orient, where he was alone in a vast land. His companions did not like him, for he was not like other men. He smoked little, when the fingers of his companions might have been dipped in iodine for the cigarette stain. He drank less—rather remarkable for one who had been an army-engineer in the Orient. As for women, they never interested him. A strange young man he was, silent to taciturnity; with but one emotional outlet. It was an error to say he never drank. He did drink. Music. Rhythm. Harmonies. Melodies. That lad could play a violin!

Peter Scarlet had met him in Acre with Allenby's outfit. From the first had sprung their rock-like friendship. The curio-hunter always looked forward to meeting Cameron again. If they chanced to meet in town, so much the better. Then Cameron would have his instrument. Together they would retire to a quiet retreat. Scarlet would demand the violin. The young engineer would play and play and play. Months of silence, lost in gray desert desolation would leave him hungering for the music; and at each return pent up seas of song poured from his heart. Scarlet would sit enraptured, puffing cigar after cigar, submerged in a fog of stupefying tobacco-smoke, lost to the wizardry of the engineer's violin. Afterward, they would both be quite exhausted.

Lounging in the door of his tent, Cameron thought of these hours spent with Peter Scarlet, and smiled wistfully, longing for the instrument.

"Wish I had the old fiddle here. Wouldn't seem so dismal. This place is like a graveyard."

Twilight hung death-quiet over the sombre battlements of El Ghor, bringing faint relief from the intense heat that had burned the valley all day; burned glowering cliff, arid beach, gray sea; burned into unutterable loneliness. The gloomy pall of silence was broken only by the everlasting slup-cup, slup-cup of uneasy water slapping the shore.

A white-faced moon peered over black crags. Tiny fires before the Arab tents farther down the shore twinkled through the dusk, and emphasized the solitude.

Cameron brushed moist hair from his forehead with a listless hand, and sighed.

"God, it's hot! If this place isn't hell, I don't know what is! Wonder where that fat Arab guide of Peter's is keeping himself? Haven't seen the beggar all day. Well, that suits me."

He fingered the rifle in his lap, and peered into the tent. The rear tent flaps opened on a shallow cavern scooped into the cliff wall. On the cavern floor lay the stone door Scarlet had pried from the wall, admitting him to an inner vault where, guarded by the forgetful years and the grim unfriendliness of El Ghor, a treasure had slept through the centuries.

Sombre sea, gray cliffs, night shadows, struck melancholy to the heart of the young engineer. He recalled stories of Egyptologists falling prey to strange spells cast by the unsealing of ancient tombs; stories told by the Arabs of phantoms and spirits of the long-dead angered at the desecration of their graves.

With a grunt of disdain at his nervousness, he fumbled to light a lantern. The yellow glow sketched wandering shadows on the tent wall; threw glimmerings over the moving water of the sea. Odd timber chunks, flung by capricious waves, were strewn on the beach. A drifting tree had been tossed up on the shallow shore. In the lantern light the twisted limbs, heavily crusted with salt, assumed semblance to the skeleton of some fantastic monster that might have roamed El Ghor when the earth was young.

Staring at the crooked branches, Cameron grew imaginative, then uneasy.

"Blast it, I'm an awful child! Jumping at noises, and sneaking glances over my shoulder. Those cliffs *do* sort of get a chap. And that sea! Looks like a moving desert of black sand; and that damned drift-wood a flock of Plesiosaurs' bones. Wish I hadn't bumped into Peter, in a way. I'd be back with my violin. Glad to help him out with his research, though, but… wish I had the fiddle… this dump does sort of hook fingers into you— And I'm a jolly ass!"

He turned his attention to a venerable copy of the *London Times*, and was thus engaged when Fazululla crept up the beach to spy on him.

More than an hour the Arab lay concealed behind a rock shelf, his beady eyes fixed on the engineer, his fingers itching *to* clutch the treasure that lay in the cavern behind the tent. The sweat of desire gleamed on the Arab's fat cheeks. Impatient oaths moved his lips.

At last the ghostly moon was sailing high, reflecting a pale glow on the chopping water. From the tents of the camel-drivers came a drowsy hum of peaceful quarreling. The ceaseless washing of the tide, the fluttering of a loose tent flap, and a faint crinkling as Cameron arranged the sheets of his journal sounded distantly. The narrow strip of white sand leading to the engineer's tent was bathed in silvery moon-ray.

"Allah's blessing! Now should be the time!"

Fazululla wrapped his robes about him, rose wheezing to his feet, and crept cautiously down the shore, to vanish in the shadows where the cliffs hung like stone curtains into the sea.

In his tent, Cameron yawned, tossed aside the paper, and turned to slap lazily at insects swarming the lantern.

"Wonder if Peter is there, yet? Devilish lonely, this Dead Sea region. Glad I'm through working anywhere near here. Never saw a place so melancholy and desolate."

He dropped back in his camp-chair, rested the rifle across his knees, and closed his eyes. Pictures of cool green highlands came to mind. Vivid memory of gay hours in Paris. Hours spent with his violin. The friendly little violin that waited his coming at headquarters in Suez.

"Some day I'll quit this rotten desert country that buries a man alive, and go back to France, or England. Some day—God! What was that!"

Cannon roar could not have startled him more. He surged to his feet; staggered in amazement.

"If that wasn't a chord from a violin—"

Clear, melodious, on the wings of a gentle breeze came the vibrant notes that only sound from bow and strings.

"I'm mad!"

And then, before his astounded vision, danced a wondrous figure, a flash of gossamer *sarong*, a symphony of grace superb in whirling rhythm that swept along the shore, and glided like a nymph to the beach before Cameron's tent.

What a creature she was! A sylph stepped from the sea!

Torrents of weird Oriental melody sobbed from the strings beneath her flashing bow. Moonlight wove gold in her waving hair, shone her gliding skin to brass, played sheen over her silken mantle. Whoever she was, she could dance! Whoever she was, she could play that violin!

Body swaying, melting with music, she floated more than danced toward the fascinated engineer. Cameron's rifle slipped from senseless fingers. Breath struggled from his lungs. His hands trembled. Never in all the world had he seen such a woman as this! Never in all his days had he heard such strange, wild music!

"A *peri*! A *peri* from the skies! My God—"

She drew him with the mad music from her bow, and the magnetism of eyes as deep as time. Against that background of stifling El Ghor night, restless murmuring sea, and stark cliffs, that silken figure with the golden skin danced like a daughter of the gods.

Cameron had never a chance. With faltering step he stumbled from his tent. The flame that burned in his eye was a mad thing to see.

From their tents, rods away, the frightened camel-drivers peered in fearful wonderment. This dancer was a *houri* from Paradise. The violin was a spirit. They groaned and prayed. They watched with eyes that bulged.

They saw the silken figure glide toward their master's tent; saw her sway, her bow flash fire in the moonlight, drawing great throbbing harmonies from the little wooden box with strings. They saw Cameron stagger from the tent like one drunk; saw him stretch his hand out to the dancing spirit.

The spirit skipped away. Enchanted, the Arabs vowed Cameron was, enchanted. And they were not far from right.

The engineer rushed forward. A golden laugh rang on the lips of the goddess. Turning, she fled down the beach like a moonbeam; Cameron racing after.

The Arabs heard Cameron's choking call, and saw the woman with the violin and the engineer with outstretched arms vanish in the shadows of the limestone cliffs.

Then those camel-drivers fell on their faces and yowled with fear. Yowled for the guide, Fazululla. Yowled for Cameron. But Cameron was far out of ear-shot, sprinting down the rocky shore, a silken *sarong* clutched in one hand, a broken violin in the other—running like a madman after what might have been a brass idol that ran, too, like a fawn.

And Fazululla, the Arab guide, a smile of supreme satisfaction on his pious lips, great thankfulness in his heart toward Allah who had given him brains to invent such a peerless scheme and luck to find so glorious a dancer—well, Fazululla was very busy.

WHEN Peter Scarlet and Ibrahim returned they found Wayne Cameron gone, Fazululla gone, and the treasure gone.

Three hysterical Arab camel-drivers, hands waving, words jabbering shrilly, contrived to tell what had happened. It proved hard as pulling teeth to get the story from them, but Scarlet, ploughing under the wild jumble of exaggeration, finally dug out a fairly accurate account.

"That damned Arab guide! That fat snake!"

For he understood.

It took the little curio-hunter ten cigars and hours of masterful arguing to convince the authorities that he had not rifled the treasure vault, or planned the robbery himself. That he damned the region with a score of profound Yankee damns, and left it forever.

He never bothered to chase Fazululla or the woman. He knew their ill-gotten wealth would kill them.

It did. The fat Arab doped himself to death in a month, and the dancer was murdered for her jewels two hours after Fazululla rewarded her with them. Incidentally, Ibrahim, the *dragoman*, not satisfied with his dividends from the affair, committed that murder, and, like his friend Achmed, was later caught and strung up by the neck.

Peter Scarlet also knew that remorse would do for Cameron. It did. It ruined him.

Once, months later, the little American curio-hunter caught a glimpse of Cameron fiddling in a foul Suez gin mill. Fiddling like mad; eyes staring vacantly, cigarette dangling on unshaven lip; drunker than an actor's banquet.

The violin looked decayed, squeaked, and was out of tune.

SUN-TOUCHED

A tale of the East.

"I been workin' on th' railroad—
 All th' livelong day—
 I been workin' on th' railroad—
 Just to pass th' time away—"

BRADSHAW REMOVED THE cigar from his lips, and with
the trailing smoke blew a poignant sigh. Sitting alone on the
verandah step, back against a mat, boots stretched lazily before
him, he let the steamy darkness finger his face, and gave himself
over to acute longing for the fresh smell of a Dixie twilight.
Asian night, mysterious and black, came rolling down from the
hills. Jungle life rustled busily among the sandalwoods looming
about the naturalist's bungalow. Green cloud cruising above
the trees reflected the poisonous slime-stench wafted from a
near-by stream more than light from the lurking moon.

Bradshaw listened. A smile crossed his features as from the
thick blackness down the trail came low humming of voices
searching key, the plink of banjo strings.

"I been workin' on th' railroad—
 All th' livelong day—"

That song sounded mighty strange in that lush jungle night;
mighty good to the lonely naturalist. And as the final chords
melted to a dying hum, he clapped on his helmet, caught up a
stick, and made his way down the path.

Drawing his automatic, he
advanced to the banyan tree.

"Whoever they are, my new neighbors can sing," he enthused, as he fought his way along the creeper-tangled trail. "If they keep up *I Been Workin' On th' Railroad* the way they've been all evening, I'll get so homesick I'll be catching the morning mail-packet out of Islamahad. Glad to have company in this dump, though. Should have dropped in on 'em this morning. Must be the chaps come to engineer that new railroad."

Abruptly the path wandered into a scraggy bungalow clearing made jolly by a crackling fire. Two boys, a banjo, and a bottle were sitting by the blaze. Leaping flame lit the scene with merry fire-glow, flickered crimson on the duck jackets and tanned faces of the singers, cast deep shadows in surrounding groves of teak, bamboo and sandalwood.

"Welcome stranger!" announced the taller of the two lads, rising with outstretched hand as Bradshaw stepped into the clearing. "Seems right good t' see another human face in these pahts. Reckon yo'all is th' fellow stayin' up creek."

"That good old southern drawl!" was Bradshaw's delighted comment on shaking hands. "Haven't heard it since I was a shaver, and believe me, I can see it's going to make me nostal-gic. Guess I'm not glad to see you. I can swear it's going to be good to have neighbors to quarrel with. Yes sir! Yes, I'm the collector camping up stream a ways. Bradshaw's my name. And you?"

"Meet Rod Madison, th' best lookin', worst banjo player breathin'," announced the tall one with a bright grin, nodding at his companion by the fire. "That's him. An' me, I'm just plain Slim Henley, th' whiskey tenor o' th' duo."

"And," continued the second lad, "we're two th' smahtest engineers come Thursday. We're runnin' railway tracks over t' them mines in th' hills. An' we like t' sing; both got girl friends back home in Columbia, Tennessee; been thrilled by th' song *Back to Mandalay;* an' have th' itch t' shoot a tiger. That's us. So just gather 'round, an' if yo' like harmony, Slim an' I'll try an' render some."

"Help y'self t' that wine, friend," urged Henley, plopping himself down on a log with the green abandon of one who had never heard of such vicious little beasts as scorpions. "Good wine. 'Tisn't th' gut-fryin' death-medicine that's sold back home. Set down. An' if our yowlin' starts preyin' on your mind, say th' word, an' we'll quit. Mos' likely you'll hear us two warblin' every evenin' from now on, but don't think we're tryin' t' torture you or anythin'. Excusin' those two little ladies back home, singin' is th' one thing we like best."

Whereupon Bradshaw, the naturalist, sat by the fire, helped himself to the wine, and listened to some of the finest harmony he had ever heard. Those two young engineers from Columbia, Tennessee, could sing! Rod Madison's soft-throated tones, deep as a darkey's, carrying melody; harmony ringing from Slim Henley's cheeringly accurate tenor, blended with tinkling banjo chords and flooded into night-hung jungle.

I've a Girl in the Heart of Maryland they sang, and *Back to Mandalay,* an unabridged version of *Hinkey Dinkey Parlez-vous,* and *Carry Me Back to Ole Virginny,* and, of course, *Sweet Adeline.*

But *I Been Workin' On th' Railroad* was their favorite, and they sang it over and over again.

Bradshaw, who had been oppressed by the morose jungle, warmed in the jovial atmosphere; smoked in contented silence. And when they tired of singing, Madison laid aside the banjo, and they talked. Talked of civil engineering, what was good for malaria, snakes, and the girls back home. They asked the naturalist a thousand questions about the Orient, insisting that he throw a yarn. Bradshaw dug one out of the cobwebby portion of his brain; told them about the whispering rubies of Jehan Jee and the Phantom Buddha of Gunong Tahan. In turn he asked them about the Republican Party, the price of theatre tickets, coal strikes, prohibition, prize-fighting, if the Wheeling Stogies were still in the league, and what was the Charleston.

Bradshaw liked his new neighbors. Madison with the twinkly brown eyes, and that all-muscle build. And Henley, genial as a pleasant day, with honey-colored hair and lazy drawl. Pals, they said they had been, since the day they were born.

And they liked the lean brown naturalist with the pepper-and-salt beard, the post-bald head, and the incredible capacity for quinine.

Began a friendship that helped the suffocating days drag by. Of murky evenings, when bad breaks on the job, and hours of thick, hot air had drained the nerves from the young engineers, and the naturalist's research had rubbed him raw, the three would cheer up in the companionship of fire, story, wine and song. Always song, at any rate. Always *I Been Workin' On th' Railroad*.

Little did the naturalist guess, that first night as he tramped back to his bungalow in the muffled dark, what grim and startling events were to shadow those boys and their song. Little did he guess. The whimseys of Asia are unexpected.

THREE ghastly horrors crawled over the baked highway, shambled through the dusty grass, and flung themselves down in the shade of a sheltering banyan. Three ghastly horrors—and those familiar with the *fakir*, that wandering saint of India, will well understand. Atrocities they were; as if each had vied with the other in effort to completely ruin himself, and all had achieved success. Filthy, naked, scummed with ashes and paint, they dawdled in the shade, the very spirits of evil.

Their leader was a particularly noxious specimen. Rope of hair wound about his malformed skull, his matted beard crawled with vermin, and his sin-twisted body was wracked by the admirable device of an iron spike thrust through the loose flesh of his abdomen. To heighten the effect, the creature wore a lady's flowery bonnet, filched God only knew where, and touched off the picture by hanging a dried head on a string from his throat.

His companions, hardly less evil, sought spiritual relief by the method of rattling charms and mumbling miles of such soul-saving dogma as *Samarthi ko dosh nahin*—the mighty can do what they please without committing sin. Apparently they believed whole-heartedly in the doctrine, assuming themselves as mighty, for they certainly did what they pleased. Their pilgrimage to Benares was going to be delightfully crammed with doing what they pleased and with whom. Their trip would he one vice-speckled journey of prayer, begging, debauchery, juggling, and any choice bit of crime that might come to hand. Saints, these men. Holy-men, indeed.

The shock that Slim Henley got when, returning with Madison from the construction camp, he found those three mendicants squatting under the banyan before the bungalow, was profound. His hand flew to his revolver, and he nudged Madison a jab with his elbow.

"Look yonder, Rod! Wow! Just look at those chaps! There's East o' Suez, for yo'. Devil comes an' sets right in a man's dooryard. Hi!" he demanded harshly. "Get outa there, you wildcats!"

Those three *fakirs* did not blink an eye! Not they. Prince, beggar, soldier and thief bowed head to the holy-man; and they paid Henley no more attention than they would have paid a flea.

"Well, damn!" Madison ejaculated. "Did yo' ever see such crust! An' such gents! Thought we saw some mean vagabonds in Aden, but these lads sure win on a walk. Get up! Get outa there!" he shouted.

They did not move; not a muscle. They might have been carved from mud by some particularly malicious demon modeling in some particularly malignant mud.

Henley groaned.

"Look at th' sweetheart with th' nail stuck in his skin. Whew! Awful! If our bearers were here, I'll bet they'd be scared blue. Run down an' get th' naturalist, Rod. Maybe he can budge these devils."

Returning with Bradshaw, Madison found Henley still sitting his pony; glaring at the unsavory trio of guests in open-mouthed dismay.

"Looks like they come t' stay," he dolefully told Bradshaw. "I can't get a wink outa them. Aren't they crazy birds! Are they nuts?"

"*Fakirs,*" explained the naturalist in low tone. "Wander all over Hindustan, and pull off all sorts of crime in the name of some fool god or other. I'll see if I can send 'em off."

Drawing his automatic, he advanced to the banyan tree. Red eyes turned towards him. The leader of the holy outfit fingered the dried head on his breast, and shrilled jargon. Bradshaw laughed. Laughed, and launched a kick at the filthy mendicant that sent him scrambling. Then addressing the three in dialect unknown to the engineers, he told them something that frightened them properly. Those *fakirs* got to their feet in a big hurry, snatched up their rags, and retreated down the road, chattering like fools.

"Lordy!" breathed Madison, as the leader's bent figure was lost from view. "I'm sick! Awful sick. Say, Bradshaw, what are those chaps, anyhow?"

"Holy-men. Get that. Holy. Dirtier and lower they get the holier they are! A special little curse on India. Few million of 'em, probably, and they knock all over the country, robbing and terrifying the fool natives. Mohammedan and Hindu religious fanatics. Ascetics or something.

"Self-abnegation stuff, you know. I've seen them buried up to their necks in sand, swung on hooks through their backs, eating carrion. Some sit years without moving; staring at the end of the nose. Some let their arms or legs rot in agonizing positions.

"I saw one up in Bangalore who had clenched his fists 'til the fingernails grew through the palms. Lots of them spend their lives traveling on a pilgrimage to some holy hell like Puri or Benares where they stage festivals that must make the devil mighty happy. Government's trying to stamp it out. They hold the natives in such great fear. Even a rajah will think twice before sassing a holy-man."

Henley fanned himself with his helmet.

"Noble country," was his sour comment. "I'd hate to get mixed up with those religious boys. Reckon I'll dream about 'em for ten years comin'. But what did yo' tell 'em that got under their skins so fast?"

"Tell us," echoed Madison, "what chased 'em away?" Bradshaw chuckled.

"Wager they're running yet. Why, the big devil informed me that if I came near him he'd cast a curse on me that would blight my wife, children, and grandchildren to the tenth generation, and make my offspring run to daughters. And there's a curse for you. Enough to send any Hindu crawling in the mire. Unfortunately for the old soak, I'm an unmarried Yankee. Came right back at him. Told him if he and his disciples didn't hop out of here in a hustle, I'd go into the bungalow, get some cow meat, and pelt them with it. Did you see 'em run?"

They had strolled to the verandah. Henley sank into a camp chair; mixed himself a gin and vermouth, while Madison shook out of his sweaty jacket. Bradshaw enquired:

"Bad days to work?"

"Slow as hell. The coolies are lazy as molasses," returned Madison. "We're runnin' over that swampy stretch right now. The leeches are somethin' fierce. After a good rain they just march in armies and battalions over a fellow. Won't have a drop of blood in my veins if they keeps up. But we're pushin' along."

"It's hell," chimed in Henley. "Workin' in th' sun is murderous, but we have to keep goin'. I get a rotten headache mos' every aft'noon."

"Watch it," advised the naturalist. "Always wear your pith helmet. The cloth one isn't worth a damn on a hot day. The heat is tough."

"It's tough country," sighed the tall engineer. "A chap hates it, but can't quit. But—let's forget it all with a good tune. A tune, anyhow. Put down th' quinine, Rod, and get your banjo."

They sang.

And farther down the trail, three wretched *fakirs* camped in the grass, called loudly on the great god Siva to burn up the white rat with hair gone from head to chin, his two companions, all white rats in general, even as he had reduced Brahma and Vishnu to ashes by a spark from his central eye.

HEAT to make one gasp speared down out of brass-hued sky. Early in the day the coolies had thrown down their tools and retired to jungle shade. All morning and afternoon they sat like rows of brown monkeys, content in idle gossip, betel-nut, and a *hookah* that passed from hand to hand. No work would be had from them that day.

Slim Henley worried, sweated, and swigged quinine.

"Rod, we'll never be gettin' this track down! Reckon we can't leave those boys lay off every time th' sun shines."

"What can yo' do?" Madison shrugged. "Th' beggars just won't labor this evenin', that's all. Now listen, Slim. You're lookin' played out y'self. Sweat just a-porin' from yo' chin. Too hot to be slavin', an' you been goin' all day. You oughta take it easy, old son."

"But we'll never finish—"

"Nobody ever finishes anything in this country, far's I can see," argued Madison with a grin. "An' we'd best go slow. You're all done out. Reckon we better call it a day, an' go sprawl on th' verandah."

Madison drew himself up wearily and motioned to Henley.

With a grunt, Henley tossed down his surveying rod, and followed his partner to headquarters tent. The coolies were dismissed, and not at all sorry, while the engineers locked up the tools and made final rounds of the newly laid track.

"It's a strange country," murmured Slim Henley, and with the words, he flung out a terrific punch.

A red globe in the sky, evening sun, beat down a scorching fire. Tatters of fevery mist hung low over the bog land. When Henley halted before a water tank in the process of erection, Madison called peevishly:

"Step on it, Slim. It's too hot to fuss. Come on!"

"We'll never finish this stretch," complained the other engineer, removing his helmet to brush moist hair from his forehead. "Never. The natives won't work. Awful. Just like those holy-men. Remember?"

"Like who?"

"Those three holy-men sittin' under our banyan tree yesterday. It's a strange country, Asia is. A mighty strange country."

Madison looked at Henley in surprise; laid a hand on his companion's shoulder.

"Quit mumbling, Slim. Come along outa th' heat."

"A strange country," insisted the other, fretfully. "Always did want to see it, I reckon. Never saw a country so strange as this old country is."

"Why, Slim," demanded Madison, "what yo' been drinkin' this afternoon?"

"Drinkin'?" replied Henley, his voice dropping to a whisper. Stooping down, he scooped up a handful of cinders, and flung them at a dump car. "Drinkin'? Drinkin' quinine. Always did. I tell yo', yo' can't hurt my feelin's. I'm a holy-man!"

Madison threw a frightened glance into Henley's blue eyes. "Slim!"

"It's a strange country," murmured Slim Henley. And with the words he flung out a terrific punch that landed flush on Rod Madison's jaw. Madison dropped. The tall engineer chuckled softly. Slinging a fistful of pebbles over the crumpled figure at his feet, he turned and fled away toward the jungle trail already purpling in dusk. Slim Henley fled away, and as he ran he whimpered, laughed, sang snatches of song, and tore the clothing from his back.

Night overtook him on the main road, an odd figure clad only in underwear and heavy boots that kicked up dust clouds when he scuffled along. Such an odd figure was he, that the three frowsy mendicants, into whose camp he descended that night, thought him an evil spirit, and accepted him without a word. Four hours after his silencing punch to Rod Madison's chin, Slim Henley, the young engineer from Columbia, Tennessee, was squatting in the roadside mud, a full-fledged holyman among holy-men. His yellow hair stank with slime. Ashes from the fire made of his underwear and boots were plastered over his body. Paint smeared his face. A dirty rag circled his loins. The old scoundrel who had led the crew, now displayed a black eye under the flowery bonnet, while the dried head he had prized hung from the neck of the newcomer.

The newcomer was one of them. So much so that the sobbing young engineer and the pale-faced, panting naturalist who galloped by on the road that night, never recognized him.

THAT railroad to the mines was finished by a tiger-tough, Irish, army engineer, who feared neither God, man, nor malaria. In fact his only fear was that the whisky supply would be drained away. A fear not without grounds, for the young engineer, who occasionally hung about the camp, seemed to possess infinite capacity; drinking too well, too often, and too much. After each paralyzing bout, the young engineer would journey off on endless tramps over the countryside, to come back sick and useless.

Returning from a trip into Kelantan, Bradshaw found Madison in a state bordering collapse.

"You've got to cut it out," snapped the naturalist, shaking his friend's drunken head. "You've got to cut it out and come with me. Yes sir! I'm going on a little shooting jaunt up in Kashmir, and you're going too! I've got a lodge up there that's a whiz, and if I'm not wrong, there'll be some good company in the bargain. Just the thing to set you up before you go back to the States. Madison! Snap out of it! You can't go back to those girls at home looking like a wreck. Won't help things at all. Now listen to me, you young fool—"

And as Bradshaw wanted to pick up some brasswork in Benares, they took boat to Calcutta, crossed the river, and caught train at Howrah for the Holy City of the Hindus.

BRADSHAW stared without interest from the car window at the jaundice-colored Ganges meandering over gray country. At his side hunched an old-looking young man whose face had been stamped with bitterly drawn lines that only the Orient can etch on to a man's countenance. Fine lines about the mouth and eyes—the brown eyes with purple clouds beneath. Neither man spoke. The compartment was alive with discomforts of soot, cinders and heat. Stuffy air burned.

Banging on its noisy trail, the train fled past stretches of paddy and grain fields, mango groves, shambly native villages, gray slopes, and startling in magnificent contrast an occasional mosque or ancient palace. The locomotive would groan to a wheezing halt in a dingy station. Droning voices without. Rattle of luggage. Jabbering natives. Whining monotones of a betel-nut vender, his words shimmering through the heat.

"Paungalowri! Paungalowri!"

The naturalist snorting restlessly said:

"Terrible, isn't it? But we'll soon be there. A couple good hotels in town, and it may not be so bad. You can bet I wouldn't go to Benares if it didn't save me a trip back. But once we hit the Snowy Range, it'll make up for it. Perk up, boy. Soon as you breathe some honest to goodness air you'll cheer up like wine. I tell you, Rod, you've got to forget that other business. You can't mope your life away."

"Oh, I'm not!" Madison made sullen reply. "But it just sort of gets me, that's all. I hate this whole damn land! I hate the sight of it! I hate the natives! I hate the sky, an' th' bugs, an' th' stinks, and th' whole damn thing! I hate it! An' I'd have gone home eight months ago if I hadn't been hopin' that some-where—somehow—"

"I know it, Rod. But it's mighty unlikely! A mighty thin chance. Too thin."

"Bradshaw, you can't know how I've hoped. I miss ole Slim like all hell. I miss him. We were in th' big ruckus at Belleau Wood together an' everywhere an' he was always singin'—"

The naturalist laid a sympathetic hand on his friend's knee.

"You haven't hummed a note since that day, Rod. I've missed it like the devil. And I've been hoping you brought your banjo along, as I told you. You're going to tune in again when we hit the lodge—"

"I'm carryin' it. Always will, I reckon. Well—" a plaintive cluck—"I'm right thankful fo' such a friend as yo' been, Brad. You're surely regular! This trip'll pick me up, I know. Th' mountains'll be wonderful. An' I owe yo' a lot for it all!"

"Henly! Henley!"
"Slim! My God, Slim!"
he yelled, snatching the
mendicant's wrist.

"Hell, boy, that's nothing. You won't thank me for dragging you to Benares on the way, I can swear to that. A vile dump. Perfect hell. Holy city of India, so you can imagine what it's like. One rotten riot of beggars and bums. But we'll only put up one night."

And furnace-hot afternoon was burning out when Bradshaw and Madison reached the sacred city. They found Benares seething with a *mela*, one of those wild religious festivals in which native zealots delight. Streets were jammed with a hot and howling press of fanatics. Sweltering in the heat, mobs swarmed the Ganges bank, yelling, praying, flinging strange curses at one another, clamoring to a million gods. Beastly stench struck like a fist from the foul water. Choking smoke from dead fires of a smouldering ghat drifted on the river. Infernal racket drummed in the naturalist's ears. He felt Rod Madison's hand on his arm.

"This is hell. Reckon we better get out?"

"We'll step on it. I've got to look in a bazaar down this way, and can't avoid it. Tell that coolie to hustle the luggage. Stick close, and knock over any of these maniacs that plop under foot. We don't want to be down here long."

Colorful streams of rags and riches straggled in the lanes. Taciturn Moslems, sneering at all who were not sons of Islam. Rugged Sikhs, Afghans with dyed beards, tall Punjabis, Jew merchants, shy hillmen, Turks horrent with shaggy hair, and above all, beggars. Here was a *devotee* squatting on a bed of rusty spikes, to the awed satisfaction of a crowd. There a juggler fleeced two old cameleers. In a dingy alcove, a *yogee* with both arms withered as dry sticks stared at the sky. A young *talookdar* with pearl earrings, an Oxford education, and a charming taste in young ladies, stared at the holy-man. Sin and ecstatic worship. Diamonds and dirt. Stinks and perfumes.

A beery old derelict, ragged as a low-caste native, plucked at Bradshaw's sleeve.

"Show 'e aroun', sir? Take 'er t' th' *Gyan Bapi* t' see th' water er knowlidge; t' th' Monkey Temple; th' gol' images o' Krishna; footprints o' Vishnu; er see th' bleedin' tree—"

"Bleeding tree?" Bradshaw shook himself away. "Bleeding tree? So they got one here, too?" Turning to Madison: "All fakes. Make Barnum an amateur. Saw one of those bleeding trees in Allahabad ten years ago, and it needed a fresh coat of paint. Rod, I'm sorry to admit there's a festival going on here. The town will be full up to the neck with panhandlers and hokum. All the devils in India seem to get in here. As scurvy a mob as a man could ever see! These riots always end up in a stiff epidemic or something that wipes a good many of 'em out."

Shoving their way down a rambling lane crowded with natives, they finally stepped out on a public square. Here an appreciative audience gaped at a Brahmin whose opium-shrunk form was huddled in the torrid midst of five hot little bonfires, sweating the sin from his soul. Unable to resist a chance to commercialize, three attending *fakirs* spread through the crowd to indulge in some industrious begging. Madison, followed by his coolie, was pushing through the jam when a grotesque hand, seeking alms, was thrust before his face.

Turning, the engineer stared at a creature whose gaunt limbs, smeared with paint and ashes, were swollen from exposure. Dead eyes peered from behind a writhing tangle of hair. A withered head hung on a string suspended from the *fakir's* neck.

"Come along!" urged Bradshaw, seeing his companion halt. "Come away, Rod."

"Wait. I'll give the old idiot a coin. Looks like he never ate a square meal in his life."

Reaching into his belt, Madison flipped the beggar a four-anna bit. The way that old fellow dropped in the dirt after it was not nice to see. The engineer turned away.

And then he flung around in a manner that gave the naturalist a mighty big start!

"What's wrong, Rod? What's the matter!"

Madison's fingers dug into Bradshaw's arm like trap-teeth.

"Listen! Brad! Listen to that!"

His shaking finger pointed at the holy-man, who stood turning the coin in his hand, and humming to himself. Humming under his breath. Humming a low chant.

"Bradshaw!" screamed Madison. "Do you hear!"

The naturalist heard! As he listened his heart turned to water, his knees went sick, his hands hung lamely at his sides. That wretched *fakir* mumbled a chant, and the words he hummed struck Bradshaw to stone!

> *"I been workin' on th' railroad—*
> *All th' livelong day—"*

Madison let out a cry that echoed above the clamor like a shot.

"Henley! Henley!" he yelled, snatching the mendicant's wrist. "Slim! My God! Slim!"

The low voice faltered. The raggedy head bent lower over the coin.

> *"I been workin' on th' railroad—*
> *Just t' pass th' time away—"*

"Henley!" Madison shrieked; and the crowd fell back. "Slim! It's Rod!"

No answer from the begrimed figure, but the lips ceased their garbled chant. Beating his fists together in agitation, Madison turned desperately on the naturalist.

"Brad! My God! What can we do?"

To save his soul, Bradshaw could not speak. He could not. Words struggled in his throat, and when he finally whispered, his voice was husky as parched cornstalks rustling in a wind.

"The banjo!" he managed. "Get the banjo. Sing—"

Then the crowding mob in that stifling Benares lane witnessed the strangest sight in all India, in all Asia, in all that vast country of the strange. Those startled onlookers saw the young engineer go tearing at his luggage kit like a mad man, dumping garments and equipment in the roadway mud. They saw the gaunt naturalist struggling with the feebly resisting *fakir* in an effort to brush the tangled hair from his hidden face. They saw the young engineer snatch up a nickled instrument with strings, an instrument that trembled wildly in his hands until he struck a ringing chord. They heard him sing.

Rod Madison sang. Kneeling in the midst of that staring throng, banjo cradled against his breast, baggage strewn in tumbled heaps at his boots, that young engineer from Columbia, Tennessee, sang as he had never sung before. The full-throated Southern voice mingled its melody with that of the throbbing banjo.

> *"I been workin' on th' railroad—*
>   *All th' live long day—"*

Bradshaw released his clasp on the bony wrist, and backed away.

> *"Just t' hear th' whistle blowin'—*
>   *Rise up s' early in th' mohn—"*

Words never set in stranger background. Never sung as Rod Madison sang them in that stuffy Benares twilight. Rose-tinted gloaming bathed the scene in warm color, glowed on the face of the singer, on the awe-stricken faces in the crowd. From some kindly retreat a fresh breeze began to blow.

Singing for a life, Rod Madison was, and the sweat streaked his cheeks, pasted hair to his forehead. That crowd did not realize it was witnessing a miracle that hung all the miracles of Oriental lore in the garb of nonsense. But it was.

For slowly a look of recognition came into the blue eyes beneath the tousled yellow hair; slowly the stupid dullness cleared away. The face paled white as mountain snow as Slim Henley faltered out a pitiful hand, and whispered:

"Why, Rod—Rod Madison! Th' song—I—th' railroad, old man! Reckon I—why—an' for God sakes how'd all this stinkin' mess get spilt on me? Why, Roddy, don't be cryin'—"

THE IDOL BREAKER

*Evil cunning of the devil's favorite son, a
mad hunt for the golden god—and Peter
Scarlet dodges stark tragedy by an eyelash!*

THE MINUTE HE swung up the rotten gangplank and stepped on the sagging deck of *Our Singing Sister,* Peter Scarlet sensed trouble. When the little schooner, heading for British North Borneo, pointed her bull nose out into the Gulf of Siam and Scarlet caught his first glimpse of the skipper, he knew that evil stalked the vessel. Evil in the shape of a skipper.

Gagnon was his name; and if ever the devil sent his favorite son to malign the earth, it was this French skipper of *Our Singing Sister.* The little American curio-hunter sucked in a hot breath when he saw him.

Gagnon was different. His bulk deceived one as to his height. Thick torso stood on thick legs. Arms thick as trees hung from Atlantean shoulders, and his little head squatted on a thick red neck pitted at the base by boil-scars. Soft yellow fuzz covered legs, arms, skull, and the chest that bulged like a wine cask. A barkentine under full sail, three winged angels, a French flag and a naked lady were tattooed across the tremendous chest. Peter Scarlet was never to forget those tattooings.

Gagnon was a mean one. Not an hour had *Our Singing Sister* been under way when the curio-hunter was startled from his doze on the forward deck by a volley of shrieks that struck into the torrid afternoon like fired needles. Clapping hand to automatic, Scarlet ran to the open hatch from which issued the chilling screams. On the steps of the companionway crouched a Chinese sailor-boy, and Gagnon was flaying him with a tarred rope. Every time the rope struck it lashed a streak of blood and the boy drew a shriek from his very knees. As the big French skipper seemed to be just getting started, it looked as if the young seaman was going to be beaten to death.

With a stifled cry, Scarlet drew his automatic. Anger cloyed his tongue. He could say no word, but Gagnon understood. His gimlet eyes sprayed hate at the curio-hunter, but he tossed away the rope.

"*Sacre!* This lousy Chinee get his head bust off if he don't do wot I say! An' you, *monsieur,* wot you playin' with is the death, huh?"

Spitting a pungent Latin oath, he swaggered away, his burly figure lost in the stinking darkness below decks.

"Lord," breathed the curio-hunter, tapping his gun. "This little friend is going to stay right under my hand the rest of the trip. It will take a mighty unusual thing to make our French skipper forget this incident."

But Gagnon *did* forget it; and it *was* a mighty unusual thing that made him do it.

BESIDES Peter Scarlet, *Our Singing Sister* carried two other passengers. Night was creeping fast over the Cambodian shore, and smoky ship's lanterns emphasized the gloom, when these two passengers showed their faces for the first time. Seated in the deckhouse shadow, Scarlet stared at them, himself unnoticed. And he found nothing reassuring in their demeanor.

One was a fat Portuguese whom the curio-hunter recognized as a shell-trader named Sousa. The fellow seemed beside himself with excitement. His coarse beard trembled with his agitated flow of words. Brown hands gesticulated furiously. He was a decided contrast to his companion.

When Peter Scarlet saw the shell-trader's companion, his nerves all but twitched him to his feet. There is something about an Oriental that can tweak a man's nerves like that. And the shell-trader's companion was Oriental—the very soul of Asia.

A monk he was, a Buddhist monk, and standing as he did, in the lantern light, his lean face impassive as chiseled rock, great shadows marking sunken cheeks and deep-set eyes, his skinny hands clutching unsavory rags about his limbs, he gave Scarlet the chills. And he gave the shell-trader chills, too. They had been engaged in earnest conversation when that old monk suddenly shut his lips with a snap.

"Blessed Mother!" squawked the Portuguese. "What is wrong? Come! Holy Saint Francis, don't stare so! You were going to tell me—"

With warning hiss, the monk flung out a restraining hand.

"Be quiet!" he whispered in a voice that made the listening curio-hunter think of winds in the lost caves of the Garo Hills. "Be quiet, fat one. We are not alone."

The shell-trader peered about in a hurry. When he finally discerned Scarlet seated there in the darkness of the deckhouse, he snatched the monk's wrist, yanked him back, and together they hurried down the companionway.

That gave Peter Scarlet something to think about. For some moments he sat in silence, breathing the hot night air, listening to the pleasant slap of water against the schooner's prow, his mind busied with the shell-trader and the monk. Nervously he fumbled for a cigar. But he did not light it. Instead, he dropped the weed and pressed hastily back into shadow.

Stealthily as a cat, a massive figure prowled around the corner of the deckhouse, paused to listen; then, making no sound, it crept down the companionway where the monk and shell-trader had so recently fled. Recognizing the bullet-head and ponderous form of Gagnon, the French skipper, it took no seventh sense to tell Peter Scarlet that evil aboard *Our Singing Sister* was brewing fast.

Surely the monk's action had been mysterious, and now the skipper's sly conduct fanned the curio-hunter's interest into determination to find out what it was all about. Warily he stole from hiding and peered about the deck. Aft, a negro helmsman hung over the wheel. A Burmese sailor on watch slept peace-fully, his back to the boat-davit. Light from the taffrail-lantern clearly outlined the two seamen, either of whom could see Scarlet or had seen the skipper. Amidships the deck was blacker than pitch.

Nerves a-jangle, the curio-hunter crawled to the open hatch, and, tense with caution, stole down the companionway into the hold. Darker than the deepest whale-hole of hell was that hold, and the minute he set foot in it Peter Scarlet was sorry. Incredible ink-blackness plunged over the curio-hunter like a cloak thrown over his head. Foul stench of rotting timbers and spoiling meat hit him in the face like a blow.

Nearby, the hull was awash, and with the sound of sucking water mingled the squealing of rats. That hold was no nice place to be. And Scarlet was on the point of turning to clamber out when a voice spoke from the tremendous dark deep in the stern.

"No one is there. I hear no sound. Rats, maybe. Come—tell the story!"

"It is senseless to sit, thus, in night," came the monk's reply. "Light the taper. We can see if anyone is about. And we can see when anyone approaches."

Flickered a match, a candle flared, and Scarlet, crouching under the companionway steps, was witness to a scene that might have wandered earthward from hell. Lighting but a few feet of that infernal darkness, the taper's yellow glow wavered on the shell-trader's greasy face and on the skull-like countenance of the Buddhist monk. They were squatting beside a stow of buffalo-hides. Oily bilge washed over their feet. The Portuguese was holding the candle. The monk's bony hands fluttered before his face as he began to talk.

Never in all his days had Scarlet heard a voice such as that Buddhist monk commanded. Never! From whisper to hiss, from chant to guttural growl, it poured out the monk's story. What a voice! What a story!

Hunched beneath the steps there in the slimy hold of *Our Singing Sister,* the little American curio-hunter forgot vile smells, rats, the misery of cramped limbs. He forgot everything. He lost himself to the imagery of that lean monk's words. He hung breathless on the throbbing story that crept out into the candle-light.

The living story that crept into the candle-light was the story of sixteen pilgrims who wished to achieve Nirvana. They were fools, those pilgrims. They were too lazy to practice the rigid teachings of Buddha—too rich and too lazy. Like all fools possessing wealth, they thought to buy salvation. And they imagined by flattering the Gautama they could do it.

So they hired five and forty goldsmiths to cast an image of Buddha out of solid gold. The image stood four feet high, pure yellow gold, the eyes set with two of the finest rubies money could purchase. The pilgrims thought their salvation was now assured and, with great acclaim, set their golden image in a shrine on a high hill.

All-wise Buddha, seeing this, was furious. To make an example of the false pilgrims, he set an aged stonecutter chiseling a crude image from cheapest granite. The old codger worked like the devil, sweat and cut his hands. Hammering the final touch, he dropped dead of exhaustion and his soul gained Nirvana.

Then Buddha whisked that giant stone image—the Orient never asks how; it has faith—into the shrine of the sixteen pilgrims and placed it facing the costly idol of gold. An inscription traced over the temple door by the Gautama's own hand told how infinitely more worthy was the crude image produced by toil than the golden one. Moreover, it warned worshippers to abhor the gold idol, but adore the granite.

Next morning the sixteen pilgrims hurried to their shrine. Paying no heed to Buddha's mandate, they fell on their knees before the golden image. A fisherman passing on the beach below the temple heard ghastly cries; he climbed to the shrine, and the sixteen foolish pilgrims were gone.

Five days later, the drowned corpses of the whole sixteen were washed to the beach of a distant shore. From that day to this, pilgrims daring to enter the shrine turned away from the idol of gold and worshipped the image of stone.

THAT was the story of the shivering old Buddhist monk as he told it in the stifling cargo hold of *Our Singing Sister*. Peter Scarlet believed that story. He saw those sixteen smug pilgrims with their hypocritical smiles. He felt the insulted Gautama's rage. He saw the bleeding hands of the slaving stonecutter; heard the pilgrims scream; saw their bodies flung up on the distant shore. That monk was a splendid storyteller.

Peter Scarlet was not the only one who believed the monk. The fat Portuguese shell-trader believed. The taper in the pudgy fingers shook so the flame almost spluttered out.

"Tell me," he croaked. "Quick! Where is this shrine? Where is the shrine that holds the gold god with ruby eyes—"

"Softly," whispered the monk. "The shrine is nothing to me, fat one. I have ventured there only once, and that time many years ago. Memory fails me, for I am old—old and starved. Yet, if the right amount were offered, perhaps I could recall—"

"Holy Saint Stephen!" snarled the shell-trader wildly. "How much do you ask? Quick! I'll give it to you!" Scarlet saw him fumbling at his belt; saw avarice gleam in the mendicant's eyes as he stretched out a thin hand. And then the curio-hunter saw something else, something that froze the breath in his lungs.

The Portuguese had raised the taper high to cast better light on the coinbag in the monk's hand. When he did so, a straying yellow beam fell straight on a face that peered from an overhead timber-brace. Gimlet eyes sparkling greed, twisted mouth, sweat glistening on fuzzy hair—that was the face Scarlet saw. That was the face that the monk saw.

If Scarlet had forgotten the French skipper, he remembered him now. The monk threw a screech that sent a thousand rats scampering, and Gagnon dropped from his hiding-place like an attacking gorilla. Down went the shell-trader, his bones snapping under the skipper's bulk. Out went the candle. Followed a brief moment of fierce scuffling, the darkness lit by a brace of desperate yells. Then a match flickered, and the taper glowed again.

Light revealed the shell-trader's body doubled against a brace, blood oozing from the mouth, serenely unconscious. Squawking feebly, the old monk writhed with Gagnon kneeling on his chest. Holding the candle before the monk's eyes, the skipper said:

"Tell me! Tell me, old man, where the shrine lies! *Oui!* If you don't tell me, I'll grind you to curry powder. *Morte de mon vie!* I will!"

The monk closed his eyes, sealed his lips.

"But you *will* tell me!" insisted Gagnon. With a powerful hand he caught that rice-fed wretch by the scruff of the neck, jerked him to his knees and shook him until his teeth rattled like hail on a copper roof. Then bending the monk's neck in no soothing manner, he rammed the yellow face under the oily bilge washing the bottom of the hold.

With a frenzied lunge the monk twisted away, gasped wildly for breath, and gurgled a dozen words in Siamese dialect which Scarlet could not understand.

Gagnon understood. Snatching the monk into his arms, he kicked at the fallen Portuguese, kicked out the candle and rushed up the companionway, his bobbed boots crashing on the steps over Peter Scarlet's head.

OUR SINGING SISTER was surging through the night-hung gulf somewhere off Hastings Archipelago. Save where lanterns bit into the murk, the deck was black as Egypt.

Scarlet sneaked from the companionway, and darted to the schooner's rail. Above the whine of straining timber, the crushing of waves against the prow, he could just hear the faint creaking that came from over the black water and the creaking of rusty oarlocks.

No easy matter to lower the remaining dory without being noticed, but the curio-hunter managed to do it. The negro steersman aft, and the Burmese sailor on watch were engaged in a friendly quarrel over a plug of tobacco. Working madly, Scarlet lowered away, cast off the sea-painter, unhooked the boat-pin, shoved out and dug oars into the snaky water. A looming black hulk, *Our Singing Sister* slid away in the night.

Peter Scarlet was alone in the Gulf of Siam, cursing himself for nine kinds of a fool. Not quite alone. Off there in the night, Scarlet knew that Gagnon and the Buddhist monk were pulling shoreward. Rowing desperately and reviling his noisy oarlocks, the curio-hunter nosed his tiny craft in the direction he could only guess Gagnon had taken.

"He's going after that gold god, and he's making that devil of a monk lead him. But I won't let him get away with it! God, I'll bet that image is worth fortunes!"

Scarlet admitted to himself that he was a damned idiot for plunging into such a crazy adventure, but confessed nothing in all the world tempted him like the sight of that gold Buddha with ruby eyes.

"And if anyone gets it, it won't be that French devil! Not if I can help it! Lord, it can't be located far from here; unless that damned monk is leading a wild-goose chase!"

Abruptly, the curio-hunter stopped muttering. An oath escaped him. He reached a hand to the bottom-board of the dory. The hand met water to his wrist.

"The devil! She's leaking like a sponge!"

Then Peter Scarlet rowed! He had lost all track of the boat he trailed, but he rowed, anyway. He rowed like mad. Blisters seared his palms. Sweat soaked his jacket, dripped from nose to beard. Breath panted from his teeth like hot steam. The little American curio-hunter rowed, and slowly the dory drank in gulps of water; slowly the dory settled.

Suddenly Scarlet found himself treading sea, waves gliding over his head. Firmly convinced that he was heading for the Malay coast two hundred and fifty miles distant, he found a little prayer in the cobwebby portion of his memory, breathed it to his God, and struck out swimming. And he had not taken twenty strokes before his boots scraped bottom. A dozen paces, and he was standing on dry land.

If he had been lost at sea, he was doubly so now. Thick steamy night clung about him like a cloak. He could not see his hand before his eyes. Sour-smelling tropic breeze told him he stood near jungles. The murmur of tumbling water betrayed a reef farther down the shore. Shaking his sopping garments, he sat down on the sandy beach to wait for daylight.

"*Parbleu!*"

The oath ripped out of the silence like a knife thrust and was followed by a flood of Siamese. A point of light glowed in the gloom. Scarlet saw a hairy wrist, a tattooed chest. Then a lantern swung full into view.

It looked mighty bright shining from the blackness down the coast. Its ruddy flare disclosed background of verdant jungle, a dory beached on the sand, the crouching figure of the Buddhist monk, hands lashed to the dory-painter, and the French skipper who had just rounded a hillock that jutted into the sea.

Gagnon's words just reached Scarlet where he lay breathless in the dark.

"Too black is the night, old snake. Blacker than a woman's curse! I cannot find the path, nor can I see the hill. Get up! *Sapristi!* If it was not so dark I'd kick the truth from this mad monk and find the shrine alone! Up, bare-bones! *Sacre!* You shall lead me to the place now! And if you have tricked me, it shall be sad for you! Very, very sad!"

Grabbing the old monk's nose between thumb and finger, he wrenched it so violently that the victim's yells echoed for three minutes afterward. That monk draped a glance over his abuser that consigned him to the eleventh depth of hell, sullenly wiped his bleeding nose, and, plucking his rags to his skinny chest, started down the beach. Gagnon caught up the lantern to follow close after, a knife in his fist. Keeping far in the rear, his eye on the beam of light, Peter Scarlet trailed them.

The Buddhist monk led way over a fiendish path. It was just that, a fiendish path, over stony beach, through prickly thickets, across a sucking swamp that sighed poisonous breaths of malarial fever and was alive with snakes. Gagnon panted and cursed.

Floundering in the inky muck, Scarlet sweated with fear lest the noise betray him; but the skipper made such a furious racket and the monk was so intent on the trail that Scarlet was unheard.

After dragging across a particularly rotten bog the curio-hunter noticed the path beginning to ascend. The rise became so steep, the trail so difficult, that progress was made with utmost labor. Only the French skipper's screaming profanity saved Scarlet from being heard when stones rattled under his boots. And a rose-tinted cloud was streaking the sky just as the monk topped the hill.

Seeing the banner of dawn, Gagnon poked the monk a vicious dig with his knife.

"Allons! Will we never get there? A curse on it! How much farther is the damned place?"

For answer, the old monk stopped dead in his tracks and pointed a finger before him.

"There! The shrine lies there. When the mists lift you shall see."

Wet, ghostly fog was wisping over the hilltop. Its gray curtain drifted between Scarlet and the men ahead, and the curio-hunter did not see what happened when he heard Gagnon's brutal laugh replied to by the monk's screech. Smoky vapors rolled by to disclose a corpse lying in the path up the hill. The French skipper was gone.

Clouds in the East were brightening to crimson. Dawn chill was passing. Scarlet could hear the scrambling boots of the skipper farther up the trail. Blazing like a fanned fire, the crimson cloud suddenly burst to a globe of burnished copper that strung the sky with maroon streamers. Heat drew the fog. Rising mists lifted veil from the walls of a stone temple, the arched spire of which overlooked deep valley and boundless sea.

To his dismay, Scarlet saw that the trail had led along the ridge of sheer cliff wall. Far below threaded a yellow strip of beach backed by misty patches of jungle land. From the restless blue of the gulf, ranks of white foam lazily crawled shoreward. Sailing near the cliff wall, a score of gulls emphasized the solitude.

Drawing his gun, Scarlet crept past the body of the dead monk, delaying long enough to see that the skipper had cut the creature's throat, and made his way up the path to the temple door. Nowhere was Gagnon to be seen. The curio-hunter did not like that. Falling to his knees, he crawled through the vaulted archway. He listened. Silence!

Portions of the roof had fallen in, and morning sunlight slanted into a tomb-like chamber that gave entrance to an inner shrine. Musty smell of dust spoke for the many years the shrine had watched from the hilltop. Cobwebs hung like stalactites from the ceiling. Moss peered from fissures in the floor. Creeping on all fours, Scarlet gained the entrance to the inner shrine without making a sound. Inscription wrought in stone above the portal read:

>   *"The stone adore—but the gold abhor."*

"The old monk spoke truly," Scarlet whispered. "And this must be the shrine of the golden image."

Tense with caution, the curio-hunter peered into the dimly lighted room.

Complacent, cheerful and blind, the gold Buddha squatted in its corner, rubies glowing sullenly under the stupid brow. Enough gold in that ponderous, bulging stomach to ransom a lost nation! The little American curio-hunter gasped. As he did so, something struck him on the jaw and he plunged to oblivion.

Gagnon brushed his hands and stepped from behind the granite statue in the opposite corner of the shrine. With a chuckle, he picked up the curio-hunter's fallen automatic, stared gleefully at the unconscious figure.

"*Vertubleu!* Any time a person beat Gagnon to the prize! Piff! Guess I cannot still throw the rock an' hit?"

With the toe of his boot he touched the sharp stone he had flung at Scarlet. Then voicing a gruff laugh, he pocketed the automatic and turned to the gold idol. Twining his great arms about the image, he strove to lift it. But he could not budge it. He could not. And several minutes later, Peter Scarlet opened his eyes to see the French skipper struggling to move the god of gold.

The blow from the hurled rock had paralyzed the curio-hunter's limbs. Strive as he would, he could not rise from where he lay sprawled in the narrow doorway. Blinding headache twinkled across his forehead, but his mind was clear. In silent misery, he watched the Frenchman's terrific efforts to lift the idol. And with increasing interest, he watched something else.

The huge stone image standing in the opposite corner began to move. Every time Gagnon jarred the gold Buddha, that granite image moved. With a final effort to pry it from its base, the French skipper clasped arms around the gold Buddha's feet and tugged. Veins started under the yellow fuzz on his head, ropes of muscle sprang out over his laboring shoulders, blood flooded his scarred neck. Cursing like a fiend, he braced his feet, strove, and slowly raised the image in his arms.

Came a rumble like the turning of many cartwheels on cobbles, a roar that shook showers of dust from the roof, a rush of fetid wind chill as a Northern blast.

Gagnon screamed. The stone fell away beneath his feet, the granite image swung into the air, as the entire floor of the shrine turned on a fulcrum like a giant see-saw.

Right then Scarlet understood why those sixteen foolish pilgrims of the monk's telling had disappeared. Right then, he understood the meaning of the legend over the doorway. In moving the gold image, Gagnon had overbalanced the weight in his end of the room, even as the weight of the sixteen pilgrims had done.

Lying in the archway, Scarlet caught a glimpse of a deep, deep chasm that dropped into the earth like a road to hell. At the distant bottom of that awful well, Scarlet saw a faint ray of daylight, and the rushing black waters of a subterranean river. He caught a glimpse of a golden streak shooting down and down and down. He caught a glimpse of the French skipper, arms outstretched, body slowly turning, as he fell and fell and fell.

A mighty sickening view, that, for the floor had dropped directly beneath Scarlet's neck, leaving his head hanging over sheer edge. With a frantic wrench, the curio-hunter flung himself away. And just in time. Tons of stone crashed back into place, the end of floor where the gold idol had been swinging upward with a speed that would have smashed Scarlet's skull to pulp.

THE FISHING boat, answering strange yells from the jungle-bordered shore, picked up a wild-looking little man with fever-scorched face, hands torn raw, body caked with slime, beard clotted with blood and dirt. The fishing boat took him down the coast to Takmao, left him with a Dutch doctor who was not always drunk, and sailed away.

So Peter Scarlet never found out where that shrine on the hill was located. Not that he ever wanted to go back there. Not he! He was simply curious as to "where the hell he'd been." He judged that it must have been somewhere in Cambodia—near Pong-som, perhaps. All the more remarkable, then, was the concluding incident of the affair.

Cheerful in clean duck and fresh cigars, the fever gone from his bones, the curio-hunter gained passage up the Lower Cochin China coast, intent on reaching Mitho, where he hoped to catch a Borneo-bound craft. When the freighter carrying him to Mitho anchored off the mouth of the Cuatchaven to doctor lame turbines, Scarlet decided to go ashore, view the native huts and possibly pick up a radio or two. As his sampan approached the beach, he saw a crowd of natives gathered about something near the dock.

"Looks like somebody drowned," said the sailor with Scarlet. "Let's go up an' see."

It was a drowned man, and the curio-hunter gave a little cry when he saw him: A drowned man who lay face up in the green mud of the beach, a drowned man on whose bulging chest had been tattooed a barkentine under full sail, three winged angels, a French flag and a naked lady!

THE BRASS GODDESS

*Fangs of the Orient gash deep, yet Peter Scarlet
matches white man's wits against their fury
in a mighty struggle for secret treasure!*

"MURDER," PROTESTED CRAWLGORE, studying the glowing end of his cigaret, "is th' only way out of it. It's a murder that'll have t' be handled damn' careful. Th' little American, his tall pal, an' th' Hindu bearer all got to be bumped off. Dead men ain't talkin' much, see?"

Crawlgore had fishy eyes that watered like an old man's under a narrow expanse of forehead. Gold teeth gleamed above a pendulous and thick lower lip that drooped over scraggy auburn-colored beard. Subjects such as murders would be expected to interest Crawlgore.

Lem Hood, slouching in the door of the tent, aimlessly spinning the chambers of his revolver with a stubby thumb, nodded agreement. His sin-pocked face wrinkled in a vicious smile as he answered:

"That's right, Crawlgore, a dead corpse don't say nothin'. Agreed we got to bump them off. Trouble is, th' curio-hunter won't be carryin' that jewel loose in his fist. He'll have it hid somewheres. If we shot him outright we might never locate it, like Butch Clark killed that ole woman up in Kasi, an' never found out where her necklace was cached. Was Clark sore? Crazy mad! We don't wanna pull no bone like that. We'll have t' torture th' truth outa this guy."

"Which ain't so easy," Crawlgore returned. "We got to work this right, an' do it careful. You're sure he's got th' gem?"

"Didn't I see VanLu, th' Dutch trader, give it t' him? Of course I'm sure. Ast VanLu afterward, anyhow. Wanted t' frisk him, but didn't get th' chance. An' a pretty price he got fer th' pearl, too."

Crawlgore's washy eyes peered like pale fires through the smoke fog.

"Good. Tha's good. Don't worry, we'll get it, all right. We can make th' curio-hunter tell where it is. He'll tell. An' you're certain they're comin' down this road?"

"Curse me if they don't. They're goin' to Islamahad, I hears 'em say, an' this is th' only through highway comin' out o' th' Blue Hills."

"Fine work, Lem. You got th' dope good. Now, listen. I got a idea. Ain't there a old shrine sittin' back from the road, this side th' valley pass? An old Hindu temple?"

"Sure. Temple to Mukkenchore th' Butter-thief God, that's what th' old sweeper up to my place used to call it."

"Yeh. That's th' place. Th' image is a woman with a kid on her knee. They're sittin' in a big stone tank what can be filled with water from a creek in back. I seen it last year."

"You got it. What's your idea?"

"Listen," commanded Crawlgore. "We'll get th' pearl off that guy an' put him an' his pals out th' way at th' same time. Don't never think we won't."

Heads together, the two adventurers plotted. And the scheme that crept out into the smoky atmosphere of the tent, the scheme that stole on gin-laden breath from Crawlgore's grinning mouth, could have originated only in the withered mind of a man smitten by the East. Hood smiled as he listened, then shoved his revolver back into his coat. Crawlgore chuckled and poured himself a nobbler of vitriolic gin.

TRANQUIL afternoon. Somnolent jungle buzzed and perspired, its lush verdure rising a green tangle on either side of the road. Sea-blue sky gleamed in vaulted arch above the tops of palm and pepul and bamboo. From the riots of tropic vegetation steamed soporific scents of jungle flowers. A hot, lazy, stagnant world.

Peter Scarlet turned in his saddle, removing his helmet to wipe sweat from his bald head as he remarked to Bradshaw:

"Hot as the devil, eh? My jacket's soaked. How you coming, old chap?"

The gaunt naturalist grinned.

"Good, so long as the quinine and whisky hold out. How soon do you think we'll make town?"

Scarlet queried his native bearer riding in the lead.

"How soon, Kundoo?"

"About ten—sixteen—maybe twenty-four miles, *sahib*," the Hindu answered. "Perhaps we reach town before night."

For perhaps a mile they rode in silence, tongues stilled by the oppressive heat; the only sound breaking that sultry quiet being the machine-like drilling of a billion insects, or the sudden foolish scolding of a disturbed monkey.

Finally Bradshaw commented:

"I say, Peter. You made a thumping good buy on that pearl. You're sure it's the real Goondjur pearl? If it is, that Dutch trader didn't get the best of you for once."

"You bet your life it's the Goondjur pearl!" Peter Scarlet exclaimed. "And there are five hundred collectors I know, personally, who would give their left lung to own it. Marvelous little relic, Brad. Quite priceless. It's the last one of that whole wonderful collection. Think of it. On each pearl inscribed a text from the *Alcoran*. I hardly think the Dutchman appreciated its worth."

"I'd hate to carry the thing on me, if it's that valuable," Bradshaw conceded. "Reckon VanLu was glad to get rid of it, Peter. I'll wager every crook in India had an eye on him."

"It's safe," the curio-hunter assured him.

Silence again. Riding single file, Kundoo leading the way, the naturalist bringing up the rear, they followed the winding jungle road. Save an incredibly sleepy bullock-cart dragging its unhurried way toward the hills, they had encountered no traveler that day. A drowsing world.

The narrow highway crawled across a fevery patch of swamp where frogs splashed and snakes went streaking through black mud, clambered up a boggy slope where the naturalist said an elephant had been wallowing, and wandered into jungle again. At the road's turn into the trees, a musty temple squatted in a palm grove; a solitary shrine brooding in the thick heat, its ancient walls the home of reptile and scorpion, its abandoned gods silent.

"It's quiet as—" said Bradshaw.

Pang!

The naturalist's helmet jumped on his head, a smouldering hole appearing as if by magic in the crowd.

Pang!

Scarlet's pony reared, danced on hind legs and flopped in the mire, spilling the little curio-hunter from the saddle.

Two puffs of white smoke rose like little balls of cotton from a nearby thicket and sailed gayly away toward sea-blue afternoon sky.

"Stick 'em high!" yelled a harsh voice ripping like a sawthrust out of the jungle. "Hands high, you lanky devil, or I'll shoot your face off! Hood! Cover that Hindu! I got a bead on the other two—"

And Crawlgore strolled to the middle of the highway, a smoking automatic in either fist, washy eyes shifting fast over his three victims. Lem Hood rose from hiding beside the shrine and grinned cheerfully over the muzzle of his revolver. Scarlet scrambled to his feet, to stand beside Bradshaw and Kundoo, hands reaching skyward.

"Great stuff," acknowledged Crawlgore, displaying a glittering array of gold teeth in a twisted smile. "Just like th' good ole army days. Now, gents, there ain't no use stallin' this party. No use at all. Lem, collect their artill'ry. Hey! Hey, you Hindu! You move like that again, an' I'll sink a bullet in yer gut. Same goes for th' rest you guys. Stand still! Now! Get them ponies, Hood. That's it. Tie 'em in th' jungle back there. Fine. Tell me, Lem. Which one has got th' pearl?"

"Th' runt with th' white whiskers," Hood called. He was hobbling the three captured mounts in the grove behind the temple. "Th' little guy owns 'em. He's th' one that bought 'em from VanLu."

"So!" Scarlet snarled. "I thought I remembered your ugly pan. You're th' drink-mixer in that hotel in the hills, aren't you? You'll swing for this, you—"

"Shut up!" roared Crawlgore, brandishing his guns. "None of yer gab, you little mutt! We'll do th' talkin', Lem an' me. Now listen to me, runt. Hand over that pearl, an' save me my time an' lead."

Peter Scarlet sneered. Fury choked his throat.

"What pearl?" he teased.

Crawlgore wagged his head grimly; his words came poisonous and hard. His washy eyes seemed to fade, to become colorless.

"O.K.," he whispered sweetly. "O.K. O.K. So you ain't gonna give up th' pearl, huh? You ain't gonna come across? Listen, runt. As American to American, hand over that trinket an' save yerself a potful of hell. No? We got to search you? We got to hunt fer it, have we?" He turned to Hood. "Lem! We'll frisk this fool, and frisk him quick! Go over th' Hindu, an' th' big stream, too. Here, you mutts. Line up, an' step into that temple, there. First guy to move out th' way gets a bullet in th' throat. Step!"

They stepped; Peter Scarlet, Kundoo, and Bradshaw. They stepped into the dim gloom of the old shrine, stepped under the wicked eyes of four alert guns. And to the little American curio-hunter, his soul a boiling tempest, his mind blank with crimson rage, each obedient step proved a glass of gall. Kundoo moved in sullen, stoic silence. Bradshaw's murmured oaths were a tribute to water-front ingenuity. Hood and Crawlgore pressed close on their heels.

The temple was cool and quiet. Somewhere at hand a brook babbled merry tunes.

The captives were stood facing the wall. Crawlgore seated himself on a stone altar to oversee affairs.

"Frisk 'em, Lem."

Hood frisked them, frisked them with an adeptness that betrayed early training. Scarlet's pockets disclosed a total contents of two dollars in exchange, traveler's checks, a knife, a leaky fountain-pen, a box of matches, three limp cigars. Kundoo, who wore only cotton trousers, owned a few *pice* and a string of beads that were not worth the carrying. Bradshaw turned out small change, soaked cigarets, a note book and an amazingly dirty handkerchief. The curio-hunter laughed. Crawlgore raged.

"Suppose you got it sewed in yer lining, or in yer boots, hey?"

Scarlet did not reply.

"Won't talk, hey? Well, I'll make myself plain—mighty plain. Hood an' me hates nothin' worse than to have t' make a long, tirin' search for somethin'. We ain't got time ner patience. An' we got less patience than we got time. So we got to torture it outa you, I c'n see that. Fine. I likes a little amusement, myself.

Then maybe you'll come across. Got that rope, Lem? Good. Tie up these mutts."

Again Lem Hood exhibited a dexterity coming only from long practice in binding the wrists and ankles of the captives.

"That's swell!" enthused Crawlgore, when Hood had done. "Just fine. Now I'll explain my idea to these guys. Turn them around so's they can see what a cozy place they're in."

The bound men were turned around, to face the interior of the shrine. Scarlet looked about with increasing interest. A stone basin, a sort of circular tank about twelve feet wide and eight feet deep, had been built in the temple floor. Like a statue set into a fountain, a brass image about six feet high occupied the center of the tank.

A curious image it was, representing a four-armed deity, the Goddess Sita, standing, on a low pedestal, and looking up at the world with a face at once silly and horrible. On the lower left arm of the grimacing goddess sat a baby, a monstrously carved infant with the face of a maniac, the muscles of Hercules, and in either fist a large brass ball.

Like all Hindustani conceptions, the idol was bizarre in the extreme, hideous and far from godly. The brass was green with corrosion. Pools of water glistened on the basin floor. Moss peeped from between the stones. Unhealthy odor of dead years lingered in the murk. Sunlight shining in the temple door looked bright and fresh and golden.

Crawlgore's face leered its malignant smile.

"I'm explainin', gents, what my pal an' me are goin' to do. You won't come across, so we got to persuade you. See here. We're just gonna stand you up in that stone tank. There's a inlet fer water back there in th' shrine; it runs in from a creek back o' th' temple, my good pal Lem tells me. Don't it, Lem? Pours in right fast. Maybe when th' water reaches their knees they'll tell where th' pearl is. Maybe when it reaches their hips they'll tell. Maybe they won't tell till it reaches their chests, Lem. Maybe they won't till it reaches their chins. And maybe they won't tell at all; an' we'll have to fish out their drowned bodies an' take a week huntin' th' damned thing. They'll be good an' quiet by then, an' we can search 'em in peace.

"But listen, old chap with th' whiskers. Here's th' good part o' this stunt. Here's th' cheese o' th' plan. You might be willin' t' drown yerself so's we couldn't get yer pearl off you. But you ain't gonna be willin' t' let two other chaps drown along with you just fer no pearl. You ain't gonna let yer skinny pal, there, drown. That ain't nice. You wouldn't do it. You ain't gonna do that—"

He thrust his red beard and pale eyes into the curio-hunter's face. "But, mister, if you don't tell, they *will* drown, you an' them, too, th' whole kit an' caboodle, or slit me up th' stomach. Th' whole three o' you will drown. Come. Hand over th' pearl!"

Scarlet's reply lashed across the evil smile before him. His reply was that succinct, terse, meaningful, trenchant three-word command that has sprinkled Yankee defiance in the varied marts of the whole wide world.

"Go to hell!"

SPLASH of running water making music over stones. Splash of the stream that poured its crystal showers from the open inlet at the rim of the stone tank. Water rising along the smooth tank walls, steadily rising, slowly rising.

Scarlet, Bradshaw and Kundoo stood side by side, backs leaning against the brass image of Sita and the terrible baby, and waited. Features squirming with amusement, Crawlgore peered into the filling basin, watched expressions of discomfort grow on the faces of his captives as the water crept over their bound ankles. Lem Hood was busy going through the luggage packs. Occasionally he would halt his rummaging to announce a perfunctory "Nothing doin'." Outside, the sun shone yellow gold.

Perhaps twenty minutes passed. Swirling water eddied about the knees of the bound men. All three stared in sober silence, stared and waited.

Crawlgore laughed angrily. Hood, abandoning futile search-ing of the packs, joined his companion to watch. Outside, the sunlight was fading. Shadows slanted in the temple door.

"This is gettin' slow," Crawlgore complained impatiently. "I'm gettin' tired o' waitin'. Ain't you pretty wet an' chilly, white whis-kers? Better come through. Where's th' pearl?"

"Go," said Scarlet, "to hell."

"Y'u won't be so sassy when yer ears get damp!"

Water slowly rising, steadily rising, creeping up to the belts of the captives. Afternoon waning—shadows deepening without; dusk stealing into the shrine. Hood and Crawlgore watching fretfully. Kundoo, Bradshaw and Scarlet waiting in stoic silence. The little curio-hunter had begun a cautious kicking at the strands binding his feet. Under cover of the dark water he managed to loosen the ropes a trifle.

"Stubborn mutts," came Crawlgore's savage growl.

"Let 'em drown," snapped Hood. "Let th' whole three of 'em drown."

"You bet we will," Crawlgore agreed fiercely. "Drown 'em like dogs. Better tell us, whiskers, where yer jewel is. We may get sick waitin' an' go away fer an hour or two."

Bradshaw, the tall naturalist, was beginning to experience considerable disquiet. When the water reached Scarlet's armpits, he whispered:

"Peter. They'd do it, Peter. They'll drown us sure!"

Smiling, the curio-hunter turned his head to look at the image; found himself face to face with the brass baby's horrid countenance. Peter Scarlet chuckled up at the brass grin of the Sita. The naturalist whispered again:

"For heaven's sake, Peter, we can't drown like rats—"

"Don't worry," the curio-hunter whispered. "We aren't drowned yet. It's mighty uncomfortable, but don't worry, old chap."

Crawlgore, seeing their lips in motion, guessed the purport of their words.

"Say," he announced, "we're givin' you one more chance. Hand over th' pearl; tell where it is an' I'll have Lem put th' plug back inta that inlet. Quick, whiskers. Where's th' jewel hid? You ain't gonna murder yer pal an' yer servant fer th' sake o' being stubborn, are yuh? You're drownin' 'em, that's what you're doin'. An' all you gotta do t' save their lives is come across with yer pearl. Snappy, now! Where is it?"

Bradshaw looked at Scarlet. He was wet and miserable, and a question was in his eye. But the curio-hunter winked at Kundoo, and Kundoo winked back. The naturalist shivered. Were they mad? Were they going to drown for the sake of a pearl? What was his little friend thinking of?

Water steadily pouring into the basin, slowly rising.

"Snappy," urged Crawlgore. "For th' last time—"

Peter Scarlet's teeth chattered with chill as he replied.

"Go," he said, "to hell."

And the water lapped about his throat.

"Good!" snarled Crawlgore with an ugly grimace. "I mighta known, you'd be a damn' fool. You lost yer chance now. We're tired o' foolin', Lem an' me. Gome on, Lem. We'll come back in a couple hours, an' drag three corpses outa that tank—"

A moment later the captives in the water tank heard the beat of pony hoofs clattering down the road. Scarlet, head just above water level, leaned his face against that of the brass baby and smiled. His feet were wrenching like mad. Perhaps in half an hour they would be free.

Water, pouring steadily through the inlet, crawled up to the curio-hunter's chin.

CALLOUSED as they were to sights of crime, the two robbers experienced qualms on returning to the shrine. Not qualms of remorse. Not they. But qualms of distaste at having to deal with dead men in the dark. Qualms of fear lest their crime had been discovered. But no one had passed them on the road—Hood had watched one direction, Crawlgore the other—and they planned to throw the corpses into the creek, logical place for drowned men to be found.

Night had draped her Stygian mantle over the jungle land. Warm breezes, heavy with perfume, stirred the palms. From the temple came no sound save the ceaseless plash of tumbling water. Three hours had fled since Hood and Crawlgore had abandoned the recalcitrant captives to their fate.

"They're finished by now," Crawlgore muttered, dismounting before the shrine. "Drowned good an' proper, an' it's their own fault. Ain't a jolly job fishin' 'em out, an' we better hurry about it. We can strip 'em, take their stuff up t' camp an' go over it, an' toss their bodies in th' stream."

Hood was in accord with the idea. He turned a shade paler at the unpleasant prospect of entering the dark shrine, but thoughts of the Goondjur pearl and the things it would buy spurred him to follow his leader. Together they entered the temple.

Hood struck a match—

And something struck Hood! Simultaneously, four tearing hands leaped oat of the darkness at Crawlgore. The robber's scream expired on his lips. Sounded the smack of knuckles beating on flesh, boots scraping over stone, grunts, snarls. Then the voice of Peter Scarlet, the little American curio-hunter.

"Get a match from his pocket, Kundoo. Make a light."

"Jee, sahib."

Yellow flame glimmered. Flickering glow revealed a panting, shivering Bradshaw sitting on Lem Hood's prostrate form; a drenched Peter Scarlet leaning over the sprawled figure of Crawlgore. Red welts swelled on the unconscious robber's face; blood trickled from the gold-toothed mouth into the auburn beard.

Match in fingers, the Hindu bearer hovered over the scene, a smile of supreme satisfaction on his coppery countenance.

Under the wavering flare of a torch, they bound the unconscious men. Looming in the tank of water, her body immersed to the waist, the Goddess Sita watched with sightless brass eyes. And the fiendish brass infant on her arm, head just above water, seemed watching, too.

"There." Scarlet gave a final tug at the cord about Hood's ankles. "It took me a bad two hours getting my feet loose. You won't kick loose for a year. Here, Kundoo. Dump water on these devils."

Dragging them to the tank, Bradshaw and Scarlet propped the miserable thieves against the brass image. The water that came to Crawlgore's chest lapped against Hood's chin. They shrieked with fear.

"You ain't gonna drown us—"

"Cheerfully," Scarlet admitted. "Like you tried to murder us. Brace him up against the idol, Brad. That's it. So long, you rotters. Have a jolly wet time. We'll send the dead wagon for you in the morning."

BLOODY orange moon climbed black, star-scattered heavens above the palms. From distant hills whispered tropic breezes, warm with the breath of Asia. Mellow night, and tepid.

Scarlet and his two companions, chilled to the bone by their long immersion, hurried through the task of picking up their scattered luggage, packing their ponies and making ready to continue the interrupted journey to Islamahad.

Further delay ensued when Kundoo disappeared, and Bradshaw had to look for him. Hurried movements soon restored warmth to their numbed limbs, and the Hindu returned; they set out, glad to abandon the shrine in the jungle. An hour they rode in sombre silence; then the naturalist could restrain himself no longer.

"Peter," he began, "I'm dying of curiosity. Where the devil did you hide the pearl? And please tell me why in God's name did that water rise just to your chin, and then stop rising. For two hours while you were kicking loose it stayed at just that level. And it poured in all the time."

The little curio-hunter laughed, reached fingers into his beard, then made a grimace as he extracted from the furry depths a little white globe that glowed in his palm—a little white globe bearing minute inscription of a text from the *Alcoran,* a little white globe for which five hundred collectors would have given their left lung—the Goondjur pearl.

"Stuck in the brush with glue, Brad. I've hid things there before. If the whiskers grow much more I can conceal a set of Shang pottery and the Peacock Throne."

"But the water—"

"Simple," Scarlet explained. "That image business is supposed to be the Goddess Sita and her baby Mukkenchore crossing the Ganges. Hindu legend says that the gods, seeing Sita cross-ing the river, tried to drown the infant. The river rose higher and higher, but the baby was a powerful god, himself, and the water never could rise above his chin.

"That contraption in the temple is supposed to represent the affair. At some annual pow-wow to Mukkenchore the priests let water flow in the tank. It keeps running all the time, but never goes over the baby's chin. Of course the natives are pop-eyed. Think it's a god. But you see, there's a trick drain pipe concealed in the arm of the brass goddess that runs the water off. Makes a good illusion, and it was fine as far as we're con-cerned. Long as our heads were as high as the brass infant's no water could drown us.

"I saw one of those affairs up in Rajputama once, and so I knew we were all right. Kundoo recognized it, too. Now we'll leave those devils standing there overnight and give them all the thrills that you had. We can send the police for 'em in the morning."

Kundoo, the Hindu bearer, shook his head.

"No, *sahib,*" he murmured. "No use to send police. You say to them you'll send dead wagon for them in morning." The native smiled softly. "I believed you meant it, *sahib,* so I went back"—he smiled the guileless smile that only an Asian can assume—"and plugged up secret drain."

DOOM DUNGEONS

There were canyons to cross on a singing thread—black caverns where queer, silent cats held sway. And Peter Scarlet was afraid— afraid with a white fear that some one would kill Ranjit Ji before they met for reckoning!

RANJIT JI'S SLIM fingers scampered along the piano keys, and a dancy rag melody trickled out through the garish palace in shocking contrast to the dreamy Oriental atmosphere of lavish draperies, ebony tabourets, brass hubble-bubbles, rugs, and uncensored paintings. Two heat-wracked coolies had spent their lives in the dragging of that piano over the mountain passes, but what were two, or fifteen coolies to Ranjit Ji when it came to his piano. Perhaps that describes the rajah.

Habibullah Habim, his Afghani servant and head crime-mixer, grunted things to Allah. When Ranjit Ji played ragtime his fingers were stirred by deviltry. When he played, plans cooked in his brain. Habibullah knew this, and wagged his yellow beard cheerfully. Deviltry promised a break in the endless monotony of their mountain retirement—a retirement requested by certain brass-buttoned authorities with a Union Jack behind them and a dislike for the ways of Ranjit Ji.

The "retired" rajah turned slowly on his piano-bench. A chuckle eased lazily from his fat lips.

"And when do you think this little American with the white and fatherly beard will get here? You tell me he will be here by tonight?"

"So his missive said—Allah send him a plague and the devil spit on his bones! Word comes that he travels alone from his camp across the valley. He will have to climb the mountain and cross by the bridge, for he cannot ford the stream now. And he should be at our gate by sunset. He comes well armed, and the British *raj*—a curse on honest men—shelters him."

The rajah's moon face beamed benevolence. He scratched idly at a fat jowl.

"I know him, my ugly one. I know him. He wanders like a madman over the country in search of gems and similar joys. His name is Peter Scarlet and he smokes cigars, little scorpion, that smell worse than the lanes of Peshawar on a hot afternoon. I met him long ago at a durbar given by the Talookdars of Oudh. He is mad, like all Americans. You recall the note that came during the last rains? From this same creature. H'm. And so he comes here seeking word of the Floating Opal?"

Habibullah nodded assent.

Ranjit Ji sighed.

"He is a fool and a wallower in the purple muds of danger. Listen, trash heap. We shall let this Peter Scarlet in. Offer him our splendid mountain hospitality. He is just the sort of clumsy bungler to put his foot in a trap even when warned. We shall warn him, and at once he will thrust out his stupid Yankee feet. You understand, father of monkeys?"

"I understand, O son of splendid ideas."

"You are a liar, a cheat, and a mocker of virtue, Habibullah Habim," chuckled the rajah, "but I can trust you to carry out an amusing plan. You love plans. You feed on them. I, myself, enjoy the taste occasionally. So show the American in. You know my specialty—tinkly tunes and charming luncheons. We shall lunch. He will smoke a black cigar. I will play the piano, which, thank the Gods of Luck, is near a window. He will become impatient. Father of lies, did you ever see an American who was not impatient. He will become impatient to stick his boots into the trap. He will demand word of the Floating Opal. He will even insist on seeing the Floating Opal—"

The rajah swung abruptly to the piano and dashed off a lively melody that smacked of his recent and gay visits to the music halls of Paris. As abruptly he quit playing, turned to face his servant.

"We will show him the Floating Opal, my pet snake. We will give this Peter Scarlet what he asks. When I play thus and so—" he struck a minor chord from the keys—"you will spring our trap."

"Imshallah!" gasped the Moslem. "Perhaps he *will* see the gem."

Somewhere a bell disturbed the drowsing atmosphere with a sweet clinkling.

"It is he!" exclaimed Habibullah, starting up. "The white dog is at the gate."

"Let the Yankee beware!" murmured Ranjit Ji. Suddenly he began to laugh. He laughed a shrill, high-pitched, girlish laugh that hung little icicles in the hot music-room, echoed in weird crescendo down the many marble corridors of that ancient palace, chilled even so adamant a spine as Habibullah's. And Habibullah, you understand, was the sort of man who could grin at a gibbet.

SINKING sensation gripped the pit of Scarlet's stomach, and he knew he was afraid. Horribly afraid. Only with greatest effort could he force himself to crawl along the chasm's edge toward the rock-shelf where the rope bridge hung. The muscles in his throat tightened. Two thousand feet of sheer cliff wall shot downward beside his very beard. Far below, in the valley, he could see the Irrawaddy's silver thread wriggling southward; could see a hawk hovering above the mist, a tiny man in a tiny field. Sweat burst on his forehead, but he cursed for courage, and dragged himself along. Along the roof of the world.

Sweeping in a wide droop across that terrific valley hung the bridge—a single cable of greased rope reaching over the awful chasm from the precipice where Scarlet lay, way down to the door of a castle that squatted like a toy half way down the opposite slope. Scarlet could see the slate-covered walls, indistinct in the gloaming. Lighted windows twinkled in the dusk. The castle seemed miles away. And Scarlet could make out a second rope bridge swinging from the castle courtyard down to the mist-veiled galley bottom. He shuddered.

A speedy and nerve-shattering method of descent is the Himalayan rope bridge. The little American curio-hunter was deathly afraid of them; fearfully afraid of awesome heights. He once told his friend Bradshaw, he had rather marry than use a rope bridge.

Avoiding a glance over the precipice, he crept along the ledge. It seemed an age before he gained the wider shelf of rock. Here the great rope was anchored to a giant post driven deep in the mountain wall. Scarlet sat down to contemplate the ghastly venture in perspirey dismay.

"Wish I'd tried to cross below," he groaned to nearby clouds. "If I hadn't sent Mardo back with my pony I'd lose nerve. Idea of having to come way up here just to cross that damned river. But I'll see it through. Buck up, you old buzzard, and climb aboard. Maybe the chap across the stream can make the chance worth while. Let's go."

From his belt he unfastened a wooden slider purchased that day from a hillman. With nervous fingers he adjusted the affair, fitting the grooved hardwood slab so that it clamped over the rope. Then he seated himself in the belted loop slung beneath the slider. In those hills a traveler always carried such a device for he could not wander far without it.

"We're off!" muttered the curio-hunter with an unhappy grin.

Breathing a prayer to the effect that the rope might hold, he shoved away from the ledge. A brief moment he hung in space. Then his glide gained momentum; away he soared over the valley. Wind beat against his cheeks, tore at his beard. Smoking wood smelled in his nostrils. His heart seemed to stop—shooting through eternity. And suddenly his boots were bumping along the ground of the landing ledge.

"Whew!"

Swearing softly, he crawled from his seat, and stood gazing at the distant heights from which he had come. A glance at the second lap of descent did not cheer him. The bridge that would spin him to the bottom was steeper, faster and longer than the first.

"One more trip when I leave on th' blasted thing, and I'm done forever," he announced, as he unslung his slider and fastened it to his belt.

He removed his helmet to mop his bald spot. His eyes roved over the hillside, surveyed the castle. What had seemed a toy from the mountain top now loomed large in the twilight, a rambly palace with two high towers and a meandering wall. An ancient lost in the grim hills, built, perhaps, in the days of Shah Jehan and Aurungzeb when the Mughal dynasty marked a dawn of splendor in India. Built as a retreat for some *Kaisar-i-Hind* who fled before the willing scimitars of an enemy.

The curio-hunter followed a path that led from the bridge-landing to the courtyard wall. Night was reaching out of the mountains and fingers of sunset ray traced spectral designs of gray light across the slopes. Abruptly, Scarlet was aware of an intense uneasiness. Twilight was flickering out. Drugged night closed in. The automatic at the curio-hunter's belt began to feel heavy, and honest steel, and reassuring. It allayed the disquieting sensation that he was being watched. He viewed the high gate with restive speculation. He startled!

Somewhere within a piano was being played. A piano—in the hills. Scarlet knew many of the rajahs were possessed of European education that clashed strangely in Asian background. But a piano sounded mighty out of place, and weird. A haunting minor chord echoed in the night. Somehow the note carried a warning.

"What th' devil! I've used a gun before—"

With a determined snort, Scarlet reached up to pull the bell rope that would announce his arrival. A bell tinkled sweetly out of the dim quiet; and then Peter Scarlet was not sure, but he thought he heard the soprano cackle of a mocking laugh.

LACK of temper had never been one of the little curio-hunter's boasts. He was growing angry, now, as evinced by the savage manner he chewed his cigar. The rajah had ushered him in with courtesy nothing short of unction. Had chatted suavely about wine, weather, and women—especially women—and gossip of the winter resorts. Had given him chills with his extreme epigram, flawless European manner, and fat, sly smile. Scarlet felt as if he were being petted on one cheek and scratched on the other.

"Ranjit Ji!" he announced suddenly. "Quit pianoing, and let's get down to business. I came here to talk trouble, and you know it! Let's talk it and get it over with! Sorry I can't accept your hospitable offer and stay the night through. My friends," he spoke sharply, "would be apprehensive at such a long delay."

The Hindu bowed meekly, touched a jeweled finger to his faultless turban. His face was an obsequious mask. In the wavering lamplight his smile was buttery, solicitous.

"I am sorry. Let us talk freely, then. You have come to me for word of the Floating Opal, have you not?"

"That's right!" snapped the curio-hunter impatiently. "And I intend to find out where it is. Three years ago, a certain English trader named Bourncamp headed up here with that gem in his possession. He has never been heard of since. Neither has the gem. I'll lay my cards on the table, Ranjit Ji! I owned a small interest in the Floating Opal, and I own a very big interest in what's become of it and Bourncamp. I've managed to trail him here, and here his tracks end! He intended going on to Darjeeling, and never showed up there. Now! What's become of Bourncamp and the Floating Opal?"

Ranjit Ji's sigh was greasy with the oil of reproach.

"That *I* should know?" he murmured, spreading his hands. "Really, it is an injustice that my American guest does me." His tone was one of injured pride.

"Hell!" snarled Scarlet angrily. "This monkey-shine is over! I wrote you a previous message and got no reply. Now I'm sick of fooling! Believe me, if you don't come through with a pretty snappy piece of explanation, I'll have the police on you quicker than you can yell!"

The Hindu smiled sadly.

"Ah, you Yankees. All alike. Hurried and bad-tempered. You pay calls to hurl insults at your host. I am amused. It is delightfully different. And do you suggest that I know something about the affair of which you speak?"

"Cut out the rot!" Scarlet was on his feet. "You know something, all right! Quit stalling, Ranjit Ji. I thought you were too intelligent to twaddle!"

"Thank you." Ranjit Ji fluttered an exquisite bit of lace to his cupid's-bow lips; stared pensively at his thumbnail, at his slim fingers. Though the rajah's fingers were slim, he was, himself, a pudgy chap with flabby cheeks, two folds of chin, and stomach a triumph of obesity. Bulging turban, silken mantle, and glossy slippers lent him the appearance of a knight of old Bagdad. He might have been the magi summoned by Aladdin's polished lamp. The magi, however, could hardly have managed such a crafty smile. That smile said: "Dog of a Yankee, I'll knife you from behind."

The rajah said: "The house of Ranjit Ji is your house. Your wish is but a command. You desire word of the Floating Opal? I would offer you hospitality first; perhaps music—I play

American music well—or tiffin. There was a time when Ranjit
Ji was famed for tinkly tunes and charming luncheons. But no?
You say no. You are in haste. Then by the Oath of the Cow, you
shall hear of the Floating Opal!"

Casually, the rajah struck a chord on the piano. A haunting,
minor note. Simultaneously the draperies at Scarlet's back
spouted men. Before the little curio-hunter could whirl about,
a dozen arms tapped him, his automatic was knocked from his
fist, and he was thrown to the floor. Brown fingers stifled the
breath in his throat. Teeth fastened in his left wrist. Hands tore
at him as he fought over the marble flags. A desperate fight he
made, but in a trice he was pinned flat on his shoulders, while
a fox-faced Hindu clamped iron handcuffs fastened to a yard
of heavy, rusty chain on his wrists. Panting, he glared through
a red curtain of fury at the rajah's moon face beaming from safe
distance.

"So!" Rage strangled him to partial incoherence. "I didn't
think you were such a bloody fool, Ranjit Ji! You'll pay for this
business! Be strung up right! Lemme up here! If you don't get
me out of this in half a second the police will be up here and
knock this dump into a rubbish pile! Let me up, idiot!"

Ranjit Ji's voice pattered softly above the mumble of heavy
breathing. "Take the slider from the madman's belt. Without
it he can never cross on the rope bridge. Good. See that those
manacles are secure, Habibullah. Ha! And now, my impatient
fool, you shall have the word you came to seek—word of the
Floating Opal. No, no. Do not harp about your friends in the
valley missing you. No more shall they miss the lost evening
wind, or the vanished moments of yesterday. But now I sent
them the word that you have proceeded to Darjeeling, and for
them to follow at once. Ah, you Americans! Anger reddens
your face and cloys your tongue. Have I not promised you word
of that which you seek? And you are angry. You choke, and
would revile me. So then—Habibullah! Skinny cow, drag the
white *sahib* to the rose well. He shall be rewarded for his tedious
journey hither!"

A brass-headed bludgeon gleamed in the lamplight. A cruel tap on Scarlet's defenseless jaw hurled him from consciousness. Night rushed into his mind. He did not know it when native hands carried him down a long and echoing corridor into a vault-like hall, open to the sky, where bats flickered and winds crooned through the stone lattice-work.

In the center of this hall, a low railing surrounded a yawning hole that gulfed deep into the earth. The rajah strolled to the railing, peered into the black of the hole, seemed to be listening. Then he turned with an imperious gesture.

"In with the white swine! In!" His smile was frosted with malignant ice. "In with him! Who knows? Perhaps, Habibullah, he will gain word of the Floating Opal. In with him!"

The rag-limp body of the little American curio-hunter was heaved to the railing. It was Ranjit Ji who shoved him over. It was Ranjit Ji who smiled at the sickish thud of the body as it struck subterranean floor.

IT TELLS well for Peter Scarlet's scrupulous care of his physique in a land that rots men to the spine that a twelve-foot fall did not kill or serious maim him. Unconscious when thrown in the well, he landed sprawling limber. That saved him violent injury.

An hour he lay twisting in the dark, gasping and tortured by pain. When the howling racket of ache cleared from his head, his first lucid thought was realization that water trickled nearby. Each move an agony, he gained his knees, crawled toward the enticing sound of the stream. His hand encountered icy water. Blindly he buried his face, and the chill revived him.

Stupid from the dismal headache, he shook futilely at the chains on his wrists, rubbed his throbbing eyes, stared like a drunkard at the inky darkness cloaking him, battled to clear his mind. Carefully he felt over his bruised legs and arms. No bones smashed. He swore. That helped. Again he ducked his face in the water. Again he rattled his fetters. Memory tumbled into his brain.

"The rajah—yes—attacked me—imprisoned—*ohah*—"

It was black in that well, blacker than the clouds that hung the River Styx, blacker than the Stygian frown of Thor, black as an evil curse. No sound disturbed the dense night-quiet save the burbling stream at Scarlet's hand. Exotic chantings of pain confused the curio-hunter's thought. But suddenly the muscles in his throat tightened, little itchings tickled his spine. That subtle sense that warns of unseen perils cautioned him not to stir, told of another presence in the dark blindness of the well.

Tense as a strung wire, he crouched and waited. Then he sucked in a hot breath. Out of the blackness flamed a pair of green eyes—blazing points of phosphorescent fire. Four—six—six uncanny tittle torches wandering in pairs through the turbid dark.

The curio-hunter's mind was acute now. Those flaring fires glowed above ruthless fangs, and Peter Scarlet knew it. Tigers, maybe—or lions. He clutched the chain on his handcuffs with stiff fingers. Fear cramped his limbs, and he did not move. A bruised little man squatting in a hell where eyes drank him in and paws that he could not hear padded softly. No pretty situation, and sweat streamed into his beard. The eyes drew closer.

Unable to stand the fearful suspense, he uttered a gurgling cry, and swinging the chain, lunged at those baleful lamps.

What followed might have occurred in nothing save a soul-twisting nightmare. Unbalanced by the chain he stumbled, spraddled flat the chain flying in front of him seemed to drop suddenly and drag down his outflung arms. With a shriek, he squirmed back. He had fallen on the very edge of a rock-shelf and those green eyes watched from below. That was why the fangs had been unable to reach him. Sweating from every pore, he lay trembling, and the pain of his fall was forgotten in fear of the abysmal treachery that surrounded him. He would have given his soul for a light to reveal his surroundings.

"I'd give my soul for a match! My soul—"

And fate answered him with a cascade of moonbeams that abruptly spilled from a jagged aperture high above his head. A silvery ray of light that broadened as the moon rose, and faintly illuminated the rock walls about him, the ledge on which he lay, and the pitlike amphitheatre below where three lissom bodies, spectral in the wan light, slunk swiftly in and out of shadow.... Three great cats with glossy pelts white as milk—snow-leopards.

Scarlet saw he was imprisoned in a cave hewn from the solid rock. At his left dribbled the stream which had lured him to the ledge away from the pit bottom where he had lain. At his right the ledge thinned to a narrow shelf that led to a black hole, the mouth of a tunnel.

He stared at the tunnel entrance, at the beasts beneath him, at the slit high in the roof that opened to the sky. If he could reach that tear in the roof, he might squeeze through. To reach it he would have to climb a steep wall, and to gain the wall he would have to cross the scooped-out pit where the leopards waited. Helplessly he glared at the leopards, at the gaping hole that beckoned into the tunnel. He was peering at the hole when the moonlight suddenly melted to plunge the cave in darkness again.

The little curio-hunter ground his teeth in disappointment, and was about to venture along the ledge when he stopped short in a gesture to gather up his chain, and listened. A stone rattled. He heard a muffled step, a profound sigh. Moonlight released from behind a cloud filtered through the opening above, and Scarlet hissed a startled oath. A white head stooped in the low tunnel, emerged like the head of a mole. Followed a pair of raggedy shoulders.

And an old, tattered, venerably-bearded ancient tottered from the gloom, to stand shivering on the narrow rock-shelf.

The voice that whispered from the hoary beard was low and odd and like an echo from yesterday.

"Did I hear someone? Hello. Hello—" It trailed away like a sigh.

SCARLET did not move. Hands fluttering along the wall, the old creature started to approach; and the curio-hunter saw he was peering from pale eyes that did not see. The old creature seemed more wraith than man, seemed like a ghost of somebody rather than flesh and blood. In all his wanderings across the lands that shelter and spawn the diseased and strange of mankind, Scarlet had never seen a being more ghastly. Arms thin as sticks reached towards him in pitiful petition. Hands were two quaking twigs. Threads of rag wisped about a body so emaciated that a breeze might have swirled it away. Legs were shrunken to the bone, and the knees bulged horribly. Beneath the withered chest the ribs showed with terrible protrusion.

A living skeleton doddered there on the gloomy ledge, and Scarlet stared with horror at the starved face, sunken, sightless eyes opalescent in the moonlight, wasted cheeks shrieking a story of hunger-agony and starvation. The cavernous, dead eyes stared back, and again that vague voice, as if echoing from a very deep well, whispered from the shadow.

"Hello—hello—hello—" very softly and timid as a snowflake from the blue—"hello—hello—"

Something seemed to dry up in Scarlet's heart. His whole being converged in a tremendous feeling of intense pity for the living tragedy that shivered before him.

"Lord!" he choked.

The washed-away face trembled with excitement. The lost voice cackled like a little girl's.

"Some one is there! Some one is there!"

Two scalding tears wriggled down the curio-hunter's face. He reached out to guide one of the thin hands into his.

"This way, old chap. I—I—"

"I can't see," whimpered the voice. "All is dark and gone. But that is a kind touch, a kind hand I know. Do you know? It is three years since I have touched a hand. Ha. Three years—"

"A-ah!" Scarlet's voice rattled from his throat. "You—you're not—not Bourncamp!"

"Ah," whispered the old man, "my name. I had almost forgotten. Yes, my name is, let's see, yes Bourncamp. I am he. One forgets in the darkness. Bourncamp. And the rajah shall never get the jewel. No, no."

The little American curio-hunter forgot his aching back. He forgot his bruised legs. His hurts were nothing. His bruises were nothing compared to the wild fury that surged into his heart as he stared at the pathetic figure of the old, old man he had once known as a light-hearted English trader named John Bourncamp. A curse shook from his lips.

Three years in this horrible hole—three years in this infernal gloom with no company save voracious leopards, no light save that which trickled through a tear in the roof—three years that must have been three countless ages! The handiwork of Ranjit Ji and his benevolent smile.

Scarlet sobbed. Three ages, every minute a day and every day a century endless and appalling. Buried alive!

"Bourncamp! Bourncamp! The rajah did this! Ranjit Ji! Tell me! It is Peter Scarlet! Scarlet! As Allah has left his sky, we'll make the rajah pay for this!"

All that was left of John Bourncamp hunched at Scarlet's side. The twiglike fingers wandered over his face, and the old creature quavered incessantly.

"Scarlet! Scarlet! A human being! Three years dead, and now a chance to live again. I am blind, and blindness robbed me of my chance for life. We can escape. Are you, too, here by the rajah's hand? We can find a way. Dead I have been. Dead and buried with the jewel!"

"We'll find a way, all right! And damn the jewel—"

"Don't say that! The jewel! You cannot understand! Do you know? Each day the rajah came to the well and asked me to give him the gem. Then I could be free. Live again. It was a maddening thing. He would describe wines, meats, life, and I? I would get a crust. A hunk of green meat. But I would not give up the gem. And I did not die. The darkness was not unkind, and the leopards are my friends."

And before the curio-hunter's startled eyes, the old man faltered to the edge of the shelf, and lowered himself into the leopards' pit.

Three glossy animals crept into the moonlight, padded like monster kittens around the aged creature's bony feet, nosed his fragile hands. Moonray slanting from the slit in the roof played a halo, a soft aura of light about the old man's snowy head. The three snow-leopards sat at his feet as he patted their gleaming hides, or scratched their whiskered chins.

It was a scene the man crouching on the ledge was never to forget. As he stared, he was reminded of a picture he had seen as a child, a picture illustrating the stern old family Bible that had ruled his father's desk; the picture of Daniel and the friendly lions.

"See? They are my companions. Three years have I lived in this cavern grave with no one to talk to but these friends. Oh, it took a long time to win them. Months. I gave them my food. I begged them. I argued and asked. And they finally came. Friends. They love me and I shall hate to part from them…. Listen! They guard a secret door that leads from this dungeon into the palace. Listen. I found the latch, the hidden latch that opens the door. So no one could ever know, I scratched a cross in the stone where the latch was hidden.

"The leopards were my friends, and I had planned to escape at night and take them with me. They are fed bad meat through that hole you may see above. I scratched a mark in the wall, I say, and planned to escape that night. But that night there was no moon, and the mark in the wall I could not find. That was when the dark cheated me. But I found the spot next day, and marked it well. But that very evening my light went out, and I have been blind, hopeless, unable to find the cross in the wall ever since.

"It has been a torture to know that there is a door—to have won the leopards on my side—to have found the door, marked it, and lost it the night of escape. Life was gone. I have clawed over every inch of the wall, but the mark eludes me. And in the palace above. I can hear the rajah playing—tunes on a piano. Three years—with my jewel—I have hidden that, too. Ah. No one could find that. It is tied in the fur of one of my leopards. And now you can see to find the cross scratched on the wall, and open the door. We can at last find life."

He babbled and cried.

Scarlet felt the sardonic irony told in the old man's tale. The terrible frustration of losing means to escape by going blind. The old man's frenzy as he clawed the blank wall. The mocking piano tingling into the gloom from the gay palace above. The rajah's torturing offers of food and freedom. That Bourncamp should have endured all this three years, and to save a gem!

"I'll find that hidden latch if it costs me my life. You can hold off the leopards. I'll go over the wall—"

Bourncamp uttered a plaintive squeak.

"But when we do escape, how can we cross the divide. Have you a slider? Mine was taken. I planned to hide in the hills near the castle."

The curio-hunter swore, and the chains on his wrists clinked pleasantly. An idea struck him.

"Don't worry. We can get across. The moonlight is fading now, and I can see the sky is brightening. When day comes, you get those beasts in a corner, and I'll make a survey of the wall. You have marked the concealed spring with a cross? I'll find it, never fear. He will throw us food in a few hours? So. We can laugh in the devil's face. Tomorrow, Bourncamp, we escape."

FINDING the mark above the hidden spring-latch was no easy task. The old blind man quavered out directions as to where he recalled the spot as being. Cautiously Scarlet lowered himself into the leopard-pit. Three restless snow-leopards snarled savagely as he skipped across the floor. Bourncamp shrilled and squeaked and doddered around the animals, keeping them in a corner. Scarlet cursed his rattling chains, and fingered the dark wall like mad. He fingered 'till his nails bled. He clawed the stone.

And he could not find the mark.

Behind him the leopards snapped and the old man whined. Each second Scarlet expected the animals to be at his back. He worked like fury, for they had waited until afternoon to start, and the daylight from the roof was dimming. The rajah had not thrown them food. He had played in the room above nearly all day. He was playing now. Faintly the exotic jazz rhythm drifted into the dungeon, and the curio-hunter felt over the wall in a crying rage.

It was only by accident he touched the hidden spring, for Bourncamp had not given accurate direction; with a throaty rumble the wall swung in to disclose a passage leading underground.

Scarlet led the way. Bourncamp followed at safe distance holding off the three leopards trailing him. The wretched old man had removed his gem from the animal's fur where he had tied it, and he chattered like a happy child as they wound a circuitous way through the earth.

It was pitch-black in that tunnel; smelled of must and age and moss. The wall beneath Scarlet's hand was covered with slime. Where the passage would take them, he had no idea, and it emerged with most amazing suddenness in a bushy clump of rhododendron in a garden behind the palace celerium. Scarlet gestured Bourncamp to stay in the hole and keep back the leopards, while he crawled out to see where they were. Peering from the bush he saw their only chance of escape was a dash across the palace hall, down the corridor he remembered as entering, and across the courtyard.

The rajah sat alone in the music room. The curio-hunter would have liked to stop and throttle the Hindu, but to escape at all they must work fast, take the rajah by surprise, and save payment for a later date. He motioned for Bourncamp to come out, that they would try a run for it.

Before Ranjit Ji could turn from his piano, Scarlet and Bourncamp had run across the music room. Galloping after them came the three leopards. Bourncamp turned to shoo the animals back; stumbled. Catching Bourncamp in his arms—the aged creature was horribly light—Scarlet kicked at the leopards, fled for the arched doorway, raced across the courtyard, his chains dangling and jangling, and sprinted towards the outer gate.

One man happened to be lounging there—none other than Habibullah. The curio-hunter screeched a wild yell. Habibullah dragged at his knife. Dropping Bourncamp, Scarlet flung himself at the Afghan. About four feet of rusty iron chain, swung fast, wrapped itself around the head and face of the Moslem, and it was a decidedly unrecognizable Habibullah Habim who dropped shrieking to the courtyard flags.

Grabbing up Bourncamp, Starlet sprinted for the rope bridge, hung his handcuff chain over the greased cable, thrust his arms through the chain loop, clutched Bourncamp in a tight grip, shoved off and soared down into the blue-white valley mists. The shocking scream that echoed in his ears as he shot from that mountain ledge was the most frightful cry he had ever heard!

BRADSHAW, the lank American naturalist, and Schneider, the beery Dutch artist from Islamahad, ceased rocking their chairs, and sat quiet—tribute to Peter Scarlet, their curio-hunting friend, and the story he had just related. They had listened quietly, and the jungle had listened quietly, and Peter

Scarlet had talked quietly. A *stenger* and a cigar—one of his blackest—and the story had been told.

"Hanging on that chain," Scarlet had concluded, "we tore over the chasm. And the iron links were hot when we reached the bottom."

Silence. Schneider stared uneasily at the black velvet curtains enfolding the bungalow.

"Ach," he complained. "Terrible, Peter. That old man taming those brutes and then to go blind and cannot escape—while a piano was played in his ears. It will leave a quinine taste in my mouth. What a jest!"

The naturalist nodded.

"What became of Bourncamp? And the opal?" he asked.

The little American curio-hunter stooped to stroke the back of a baby *mias* playing on the verandah, before answering:

"Shock of freedom killed him, poor old chap. He died the second night, before I could get him to an outpost. He died, and I made a little grave and buried him there in the heart of the hills where he had lain buried so long. And the jewel I buried with him. You see, it was his. Sacrilege to take it. So I buried him—and his jewel—in the hills—"

A vagrant breeze whispered in the palms.

"And that damned rajah?" growled the Dutchman.

Scarlet chuckled. "There was a fearful shriek," he said.

RANJIT JI had been sitting at his piano, his slim fingers scampering over the keys picking out tinkly tunes. As the escaping men, trailed by the bewildered leopards, had scurried from the garden and run across the hall, he had whirled about in dismay.

He saw the curio-hunter and the old man vanish through the archway. More—he saw the stabbing eyes of the snow-leopards. And those same stabbing eyes saw him. His heart had turned to water. His cupid's-bow lips had given vent to a piercing scream.

The rajah's slim fingers had been playing tinkly tunes. Though the rajah's fingers were slim, he was, himself, a pudgy chap with two folds of chin and stomach a triumph of obesity. The rajah, whose specialty had always been tinkly tunes and charming luncheons, made a charming luncheon for three hungry snow-leopards.

Rajah's Opal

Here are a few lines from Theodore Roscoe in regard to the pact incidents behind *Doom Dungeons*. You'll be glad to know, incidentally, that there are more Peter Scarlet yarns coming in future issues of *Action Stories*.

India. A strange, enigmatical country breathing of mystery and weird peoples and the bizarre. Redolent of the breath of the Orient. The soul of Asia, steeped in the magic spell of the East....

It was not so long ago that my own family came out of India after two generations of living there. And they brought back with them, on their return to this West that seems to have both feet so smugly on the ground, the memories of the mystery, weird peoples, bizarre. They brought back stories.

Of these, the story of *Doom Dungeons* was drawn in part from an adventure that befell my uncle. The family penchant for adventure was born strong in him; the old home in the Himalayas was a place where adventures could be found. While living there, the family became quite friendly with one of the native princes (from whom I drew the character Ranjit Ji), and my uncle was invited to visit the fellow's palace. These rajahs were what might be known today as pretty smooth boys, not lacking in western education and manner, but often goodly apples with rotten hearts. I have in my possession the account my uncle wrote of this visit for a British publication. From this account I was able to extract some of the local color (never having dined with a Rajah, myself).

The plot of the old man buried so long in the hills comes from no more distant a source than my father, who tells a

similar tale of a man entombed for years deep in those mountains. And before scoffing the incidents down, be kind and
remember the ancient apothegm about truth being stranger
than fiction.

THEODORE ROSCOE

THE THIRTEENTH KNIFE

Hidalgo followed a knife trail that was marked by thirteen soldier tombs and blazed with steel's singing fury.

THE FIGHT STARTED in Ferussac Loti's *Cafe du Riant Matelot*—logical place, it would seem, for all fights in town to start. And Stabbin' Bob Billingsgate started it. The first and the last thing Ferussac Loti knew about it was when a badly aimed absinthe decanter arched up out of the tobacco haze and smashed to smithereens on his bald pate. Blood streaking his cheeks, the cafe proprietor sank in whirly chaos as uproar tumbled over the room.

Rose a frantic shoving and shouting and scrambling. In a trice a heaving ring of men had formed around the combatants who materialized as a wolf-faced Yemenite cameleer, and that peerless ruffian half-breed, Stabbin' Bob. Under a lethal fog of smoke and dope fumes the fighters circled slowly, seeking an opening.

In the fist of each was a dagger. In the eye of each was death.

Weapon at hip, the Moslim footed a wary path, his button eyes sprinkling hate at his grinning adversary. Stooped in a half-crouch, naked shoulders gleaming with sweat, bare feet weaving a treacherous advance, the big half-breed courted attack. The Moslim would strike like a snake—slip in and slash. The half-breed, knife waving before his wicked leer, would strike like a tiger—rush and stab.

A cruel killer was this Stabbin' Bob, feared and fought and famed for infamy on many an Asian coast—famed as a master of knife-play. A brute of a man, with arms and shoulders out of all proportion to his bowed, stumpy legs, a stub of head close-shaved, a narrow, vicious forehead with shaggy brows. His soul was as shrunken as the withered mangoes that die on stunted trees.

Smoke wreathed low. Oaths in twenty tongues winged up from the greasy, sweaty ring of faces quirking joyously in the fitful lamplight. The Moslim glided cat-like. Crouching, smirking, waving his knife, Stabbin' Bob toyed for the clash.

Peter Scarlet, the little American curio-hunter, Wilhelm Schneider, fat German artist from Islamahad, and Jiminez Hidalgo, an artist friend of Schneider's, had been sipping *stengahs* at an alcove table when the fight began. Scarlet's impulse had been to dash for the door, but the stairway wandering out of the dive had been promptly jammed with a squirming press of devils anxious to watch the fray. Nothing for it but the three visitors must see it through.

"Use your gat quick if there's a free-for-all!" the curio-hunter shouted above the clamor. "Too late to beat it now."

They climbed atop their table, and from the shelter of the alcove commanded a good view. Schneider was twitching with excitement, his chubby face sweating and smiling.

"*Gott im Himmel!*" he popped. "Look at that skinny Arab's eyes, Peter! Wow! How he hates the big chap. *Ach!* Those knives flash quick—"

"It's the Moslim's last fight I'm betting," Scarlet growled. "That big demon will knife him to ribbons!"

"*Nein*, Peter. He grins but he is nervous. See how the Arab slips away. Shades of Fredrich Wilhelm, look at those knives! Ouch! Some one will get cut!"

The ring of men pressed closer. The fighters danced fast. Darting tongues of flame, their knives glinted fire. Once they struck with a clang that sprayed a thousand sparks. *Zang!*

"Haaaaa," moaned the crowd.

"*Ach!*" Schneider steamed the exclamation.

"Moslim's going to be killed," came Scarlet's comment. "Not a chance. Do you know who the half-breed is? Yes. Biggest devil on the coast. Stabbin' Bob they call him—Stabbin' Bob Billingsgate. The police—"

A hand pulled the curio-hunter's sleeve. It was Schneider's friend, the artist called Jiminez. He had been forgotten in the seething atmosphere; had been watching the fight in silence. Now he seemed strung with intensity, spoke in a tone that tickled the nerves of Scarlet's spine.

"Who, please?" he asked. "Who is that man?"

"Why, a half-breed wharf rat," the curio-hunter replied, startled, "Known as Stabbin' Bob. Stabbin' Bob Billingsgate—"

"Ah!" The artist's face seemed to grow bright and sharp. Words that followed slapped Peter Scarlet like a blow. "It is time, then, for this fight to stop. I shall stop it!"

He cleared his throat, and raised his hand. Scarlet made a futile grab at his arm.

"Great Lord, man, don't butt into—"

"Stop!"

Crashing from the young artist's lips that command plunged into the mumble-jumble, snapped the tension of the battle-taut room, shattered the nervous wires in the minds of the fighters. It burst like a bomb in a tomb. Every eye flung to the table in the alcove. Stabbin' Bob and the Yemenite cameleer froze in their tracks—stared in amazement. A fierce, breathless silence welled over the *Cafe du Riant Matelot*—a deadly silence.

The room's glance burned at Peter Scarlet, at Schneider, and at the slight, obscure figure in the gray cloak and pulled-down felt hat who stood with raised hand, then bowed as if to an audience of critics at afternoon tea, flourished off his hat, and in a voice at once apologetic and commanding, murmured:

"If the Moslim gentleman will allow me, I will finish the fight!"

OUT OF the Mediterranean country had come this Jiminez Hidalgo, with a box of painted pictures, a washed-out face, a wistful smile, a personality as quiet as the gray cloak forever mantling his slight frame. Wilhelm Schneider had met him in the artist's rendezvous at Penang, had drunk *stengahs* with him, and found him a chap with infinite capacity for liquors and infinite ability with brush and pencil.

"I am Jiminez," the young man had said in his easy way. "A bad artist and a drawer of little pictures."

And that was all the German ever learned of him. Reserved and aloof, he went his way alone, always wearing the flowing gray mantle and pulled-down hat no matter the heat or rain.

"This Jiminez," Schneider told Scarlet, "is one splendid fellow. *Ja*, he is. But my! how quiet. And always going away for somewhere—Japan, Bokhara, Suez. Comes back as still as the mouse, but with a hundred pictures of faces and things that are mighty good. Who knows what else he does? Five years have I been his friend, and yet I know him not. Believe me, there is something about him, too. Something—can you feel it? *Ja!* Creepy. Creepy as that old hag of a fortune teller down on the Street of the Yellow Camel. I know! Like an unseen person in the room—that feeling. *Himmel!* There are times when he sits and smiles so nice and quiet that I could just yell! But the boy is an artist. Shades of Friedrich Wilhelm, yes! That Jiminez can draw!"

People saw the gray-cloaked figure and forgot him as one of that derelict army drifting over the magic palm of Mother Asia. Peter Scarlet had forgotten him until reintroduced by Wilhelm Schneider that night in the *Cafe du Riant Mafelot*. But the little American curio-hunter never forgot Jiminez again.

"**IF THE** Moslim gentleman will permit me. *I* will finish the fight!"

Said with suffocating unconcern, each word wrapping a paralysis about the minds of those hearers who understood. Those failing to know the language realized that something mighty unusual was trembling in the air. Hatchet-faced mongrel, bleareyed Hindu coolie, sea-dog, beachcomber, Arab trader, and beggar stood dumb. It was Schneider who shot the quiet to little pieces.

"*Lieber Gott!*" he shrieked. "Jiminez! Peter, grab him! What is the fool doing?"

Jiminez sprang lightly from the table; started pushing through the crowd. Men fell away, and a path opened up before him. Recognizing a chance to evade doom, the Moslim had melted from the room, unnoticed. Stabbin' Bob Billingsgate waited petrified with surprise, knife in numb fist, features twisting.

Drawing automatic, Scarlet started after the gray cloak. Jiminez flung a restraining hand.

"Please. My affair, Señor Scarlet. But if you can hold the mob back—why, *gracias*."

Wherewith Jiminez stepped up to the amazed half-breed, doffed his hat, bowed slightly, and slapped the big ruffian a stinging smack across the mouth. The room roared. Battle was instantaneous.

Fury wrenching over his face, Stabbin' Bob lunged a thrust at Jiminez that should have cut the little man in half. Metal glinted…. Clang of steel—a shower of sparks! A knife swirled high in the room—fell into the mob. Stabbin' Bob Billingsgate stood disarmed.

The room shook with the yelling. Stabbin' Bob disarmed—and by a meek-faced stranger in a gray cloak, who had produced a knife so quickly that no eye saw it done. A sweep of his hand, and the knife had been there. Yow! Moslim, Hindu, Russian Turkoman, Dutch and Chinese tongues clamored applause. Stabbin' Bob—the notorious and hated Stabbin' Bob—stood disarmed.

"Lord!" croaked the curio-hunter. "Did you see that!"

"*Er lebe hoch!*" murmured the German reverently. "That boy can do more things than draw pictures. Look at the big brute! My! I guess he was surprised—"

Jiminez spoke words that dripped like ice. A long, slim blade gleamed in his hand. Pressing the blade against Stabbin' Bob's thick, red neck he pushed the half-breed backward step by step until the raging man stood helplessly against a wall.

"So, *amigo*. Stabbin' Bob is it? No doubt a well earned name, Stabbin' Bob. Had it not been for my companions who knew you, I should never have guessed. You have changed. And now a man of knives, eh? Stabbin' Bob Billingsgate, the man of knives. Good. We shall talk more of knives."

Purpling with fury, the half-breed stood against the wall and strove to control the dynamite that pounded in his breast. For Stabbin' Bob knew that one false move and this quiet little man in the gray cloak would cheerfully sever his jugular vein. A situation to drive the raging half-breed mad. His pulpy lips writhed. His fists knotted to twin mallets.

"Damn yer!" he managed, his voice rumbling like thunder after rain. "Curse yer soul! Yer'll git ground t' muck fer this stickin' yer finger inta pie! Wot call yer got fer this?"

Jiminez did not seem impressed.

"Grind me, then, *amigo mio*," he retorted sweetly. "Grind me, then. Oh, yes. Just flex a muscle toward me and I'll slice your head clean off, by the bones of San Fermin, I will! Listen!"

Stabbin' Bob listened. The mob listened. Wilhelm Schneider listened; and so did Peter Scarlet. Silence stifled the smoke-hung room. One could hear the splutter of the oil lamps, the scurrying *chipkillis* on the walls.

"Listen, *companeros*. We will have a little game. You, and I, and Señor Stabbin' Bob. Draw away a pace, and watch. It will be an interesting game. I shall play it with our friend who stands against the wall."

Knife poised, Jiminez retreated slowly from the half-breed.

"Do not move, Stabbin' Bob," he warned. "One move will mean death. One little move—and *zip!*—the knife in the stomach. A favorite game of mine, knife throwing. A splendid pastime. Believe me, I can throw it. So I've been told. And now, *amigo*, the game. Stand very still."

The crowd had cluttered together in a solid block, Scarlet and Schneider watching from the front line. Tropic heat sizzled over the room, for the punkah-swingers had abandoned their sleepy fans to watch. Choking breaths of smoke wisped in the yellow lamplight. To Peter Scarlet the room seemed full of faces and stary eyes and gassy breathing. The wild countenance of the cornered half-breed was in awful contrast to the gentle smile playing over the artist's lips. Jiminez never wavered his intense gaze from Stabbin' Bob's face. His smile broadened.

With a sudden gesture he unhooked the gray cloak at his throat. The mantle fell to his boots. A gusty sigh escaped from the watchers—a German oath—a Yankee curse. A weird snarl from Stabbin' Bob.

Unmantled, the young artist looked smaller than ever, but not less significant. A white silk shirt he wore open at the throat, and plain duck trousers. And what held the eye of the mob was the foot-wide leather belt girdling his middle, and the gleaming battery of knives that grinned like teeth from their sheaths in that leather belt.

"On with the game!"

EXERTING a tremendous effort that screwed his features into an incredible twist of hate and fear, Stabbin' Bob recovered some of the bravado that had won him laurels in villainy.

"Say!" he snarled, his voice a mere husk. "Wot's yer game, yuh lousy monk! Tryin' ter scare me, huh? Who d'yuh think y'are? I'm askin' yer! Who are yer? Wot's yer game?"

Jiminez chuckled.

"I? I am an Argentinian, *amigo,* and Jiminez is my name. My game? I am an artist, a drawer of little pictures."

Stabbin' Bob forced a harsh laugh.

"Artist fella, huh? Drawer o' pichers—"

The words mixed into a shrill squawk. Jiminez flipped his hand. A knife streaked from his fingers; sank quivering in the wall at Stabbin' Bob's shoulder. The artist's command came hard.

"Stand still! Stand still, Stabbin' Bob Billingsgate! It will save your life!"

A mere motion to his hip, and the artist had another knife in his hand.

"Careful!" he warned, crisply.

And *zing!* The second knife skimmed to the wall, trembling at the half-breed's other shoulder. The mob yelled then. The German artist yelled. Peter Scarlet yelled. Never had they seen such knife throwing. Never!

Jiminez was smiling, with a third knife shimmering in his fingers. Stabbin' Bob was cringing with terror, sounds gurgling deep in his throat.

You have seen the knife-thrower of the circus, the knife-thrower of the stage who stands close and flings heavy blades at a man backed against a wooden slab. Measuring their shots, they throw with painful care, and their knives miss flesh by a good two inches as they outline the man against the slab. Not so with Jiminez, the Argentinian artist of the quiet smile and gray cloak. He threw like lightning. *Zing—zing—zing!* And the blades missed by quarter of inch. They shaved flesh. They stabbed deep into the wall.

Zing! A knife at Stabbin' Bob's right elbow. *Zang!* A knife shivering at his left elbow. *Zing—zing!* One at either hand. *Zing—zing!* One at either hip.

Like that....

The half-breed panted, and sweat streamed down his jowls. The stifled room panted, sweated. Schneider's good German face glistened a big moon blank with astonishment. Peter Scarlet cursed and stared and the perspiration wet his beard. Only the Argentinian did not sweat. He smiled, and threw knives. He threw those knives as calmly as if he were drinking wine, neither faltering nor failing.

Sweep of his hand, flash of steel, song of the blade twinging in wood.... He threw them like a master.

Breath moaned from Stabbin' Bob's lungs. His face went livid; his tongue clove. Fear trapped and froze him: he did not move, and that alone saved his skin.

Twelve knives Jiminez flung. Twelve knives stuck in the wall outlined the body of Stabbin' Bob from naked shoulder to naked heel—six knives on a side.

"And now, *companeros*—"

From its sheath in the leather girdle Jiminez slid the last knife; held it up for inspection. In all his days of relic hunting over Asia, Peter Scarlet had never seen a blade like this one that gleamed in the haze: A slender blade that beamed like a heated wire—a wicked instrument of death with a wrought handle of blue bone. As he stared at it, Peter Scarlet knew that the knife could speak of ages long vanished, of the bleeding days of the Sassanid Empires, when such weapons stabbed home the religions of Mani and Zoroaster. Peter Scarlet would have traded his right eye for that knife.

"Where," gasped the little curio-hunter, "did you find that blade?"

Jiminez smiled and nodded, and fastened a chill glare on the trembling figure outlined by knives against the wall.

"I found it," he answered, "in the heart of my father."

ROWS of grinning faces leering through the smoke fog—rows of sweaty, evil faces, yellow and brown and gray; faces of that gentle gang who waited in the throbbing atmosphere of the *Cafe du Riant Matelot* and watched the knife that the young Argentinian artist had found in the heart of his father. Jiminez was smiling very brightly.

"The game is not yet over—not quite done. In my hand lies the last, the thirteenth knife—a priceless weapon, and sharp. I know, and Señor Stabbin' Bob Billingsgate knows that with a flick of my wrist I could send it spearing into his ribs. And he knows I could do it with perfect justice. But it would hardly be an even affair. It would not give Señor Bob a fair chance. First, then, let me tell a brief story.

"You all know the Foreign Legion—*Le Legion Etrangere?* Of course. One deadly day of awful heat, thirteen of these adventuring soldiers lost themselves in the Sahara. Lost!...

Water running low, guns weighing a ton—beating, drumming sunlight that burned the eyebrows on a man…. A cauldron of red-hot sand and glare that boils the eyes in the sockets, bakes the skin, heats the blood in the veins, tears out the lungs—that is Sahara. And we were lost. My father and I had joined the legion together, and we were of those thirteen lost men.

"At last all weapons were flung away with hampering baggage. They were desperate, those thirteen. Holy Mother it was one terrible bake! Each man kept only a knife. Twelve of them carried regulation army knives. One big fellow, an ox of a man who left bad tastes in the mouth of those he passed, carried a long knife with a blue bone handle. A mean pair, that man and his knife; he had joined with some other riffraff from Asia.

"We had crawled to a halt beside a dry water pocket. Night came up and the men lay down for sleep. The last canteen of water was given my father to hold. My father was gray of hair and they knew he could be trusted not to gulp the water. And I was chosen to go on short search for a chance spring….

"An hour I was gone, and when I returned, eleven men lay stabbed to death under the stars. The canteen of water was gone with the assassin. And deep in my father's heart I found the knife.

"I? I collected the knives of the eleven slain men. My own made twelve, and the knife in my father's heart made thirteen. I was crazy as I fled away, but I had found water and managed to reach Biskra. I? Only my patron Saint knows the oath of vengeance I swore under that iron night sky of Sahara. I searched like mad, but the assassin had vanished.

"So I returned to Argentina; to my old home. I lived with the pampas cowboy; became a *gaucho*. You have heard of the *gaucho?* They are the masters of knife-play, and I had to learn. They drilled and beat it into me. Four years of knives with the kings of knives. The *gaucho's* knife can beat a bullet.

"I? Back to the Orient. Back to live by my mean art, and seek my father's killer. And, now, the cream of the jest. The villain who owned that thirteenth knife and vanished that night on Sahara was the son of an Arab woman and a British soldier named Billingsgate!"

The room whined.

Jiminez raised the knife and hurled it. It sang, through the smoke, missed the crown of Stabbin' Bob's head by a hair's-breath, and embedded itself in the wall.

Should the traveler to that little town in Oman chance to be cursed with a guide, that guide will surely take him to the *Cafe du Riant Matelot* of which a certain Ferussac Loti, French and fat, is proprietor. The guide will lead him to the *Cafe du Riant Matelot* to show him a design of knives sticking in the wall—twelve knives, that represent the outline of a man. The guide—who is sure to have one eye, fleas, and a dying mother to support—will point out that the knife-marking outline to the top of the man's head is missing. A scar shows where that knife stuck in the wall, but that thirteenth knife is gone. And the guide will consent to tell the traveler, for a purely nominal fee, the story of these rusting blades, and what became of that thirteenth knife.

JIMINEZ folded his arms, and eyed the cowering half-breed.

"And now, *companeros,* there stands your Stabbin' Bob Billingsgate. It is not pleasant to have stood thus and let oneself be target for flung knives, nor yet be accused of murdering. Perhaps Señor Stabbin' Bob will complain."

Stabbin' Bob did complain. He saw a huddle of delighted faces. He saw a clear stairway. He saw Jiminez weaponless. Rolling his eyes upward, he could see the blue bone handle of the thirteenth knife jutting over his head.

Crackling a savage curse through pulpy lips, the half-breed made a sudden snatch at the blue bone handle—jerked the knife from the wall. Jiminez had stooped to pick up his gray cloak. Stabbin' Bob threw with all his might at the figure bowed over the cloak. He threw, and fled for the stairway.

Up swirled the gray cloak, trapping the knife harmlessly in the sweeping folds. An old *gaucho* trick. Jiminez had expected the attack.

The escaping half-breed was racing up the stairs. Jiminez grabbed the slim blade, poised it in his fingers, and let fly. Streaking like a white-hot bolt, the knife sang across the room. A shriek from the crowd. A shriek from Stabbin' Bob....

In the thick, red neck of the half-breed, that hurled knife drove up to the hilt of blue bone. Down crashed the killer to his knees, sagged forward, sagged back, slumped to a ridiculous sitting posture on the steps, where, face foolish in death, he seemed to stare in outraged surprise at the blood that bubbled from his throat.

"Haaaaa," moaned the room.

Snapped Peter Scarlet's favorite Yankee oath.

"*Ruhe er in Frieden,*" broke in the German, with a silly groan.

Jiminez bowed, and fastened the cloak about his shoulders. For the first time his voice faltered a trifle.

"Bury him with the knife in his neck," he appealed. "Bury him with the knife in his neck so that he may carry memory of his work to his grave. Bury him with the knife in his neck to please one Jiminez Hidalgo, an Argentinian, an artist, a drawer of little pictures—" he waved a hand at the knives sticking in the wall—then at the weird figure on the stairs—"and a drawer of traitor blood."

It was even so that they buried him.

SCUM OF THE EAST

FACE UP, HE lay spraddled in the dust where the weight of a burden of native liquor, betraying his legs, had brought him down. A kindly casuarina tree shadowed his thin body, but a shaft of savage sunlight dropped full on his gaunt countenance, a countenance startling in its decay. The tangled stack of dust-powdered hair that protected his skull from the heat had not been trimmed for many months. The skin, deeply furrowed, was the color and texture of parchment. Red-lidded eyes were sunk in shadowy wells; deep caverns had been scooped beneath each cheek bone. A scrubby beard, maculated with betel-nut juice, crawled over the sagging jaw, avoiding the jagged white scar that was scribbled down the left side of the chin. The mouth, twisted by the scar, leered open to reveal gums set with stubs of black bone. Bent by a lusty punch, the nose leaned towards the right. It was a veiny nose.

It was the face of a man gone aged in his prime. It was the face of a man withered and scorched and contorted by a violent dance with debauch. It was a face that mirrored a shriveling soul.

And the body was no less mean. Rents in the tattered garments exposed an outline of ribs on a horribly emaciated chest: worn, rail-thin limbs. The ankles, poking from the cuffs of the ragged pants, might have been bony sticks. The thin bare feet, shod with dried mud, were flattened as grotesquely as those of a clown. The hand that lay on the chest resembled more a twig.

Drugs had stolen the flesh from those recumbent bones. Fevers had wasted the skin. Drink and the devil had done for the rest. Once a white man, a scarecrow sprawled beneath that casuarina tree. A sober-faced monkey perched on a limb above reviled scornfully. A passing bullock cart raised disdainful dust to shift on the skinny frame. A mongrel slunk over to sniff the twig-like hand; scuttled away.

Scum. That was the only name by which this abandoned derelict was known to the community; and he wore his name well.

"DANGEROUS?" Wilhelm Schneider, the beery Dutchman from Islamahad uttered a grim laugh to augment the frown on his moon-round face, and repeated the query. "You ask is it so dangerous? Is sticking the head between the jaws of a hungry tiger dangerous? Is stepping barefoot on a sleeping krait? Ja!

So, then, is a journey into that back jungle. Tigers and fevers and mangrove swamps alive with crocodiles are in there. And vermin and poisonous insects, and pythons that could squeeze the life from an elephant. And heat. *Himmel!* what heat."

Grunting, the pudgy Dutchman wiped sweat from his chin. "That is not all. Those little things are bad enough, but there is Tok Jangut. Maybe you have not heard of Tok Jangut. In Malay that means Old Man With a Beard. Ja! Perhaps he is old with a beard, but it is no mark of benevolence. Gott, no! Compared to Tok Jangut the tiger and the poisonous snake are nice friends. His beard, it hides the blood of a thousand crimes that spot his soul. The devil is his favorite brother, and his gang of marauders are scorpions every one. To go into the jungle where they hide—well, there are more pleasant ways of dying. I should say so! I guess it would be dangerous!"

The girl got to her feet. Shadowed though it was by fatigue, her face wore an inflexible expression of resolve. There was constancy and determination in the set of her mouth; courage in the lift of her chin.

A warm breeze off the bay stirred tendrils of moist hair curling on her forehead. Her eyes, blue and dark, stared at the wrinkling water; then sought the bilious face of lush-green, flourishing, steamy jungle that hedged the inlet. The breeze stirring her hair was freighted with the perfume of decaying vegetation—torpid, oppressive. Oppressive torpor was in the cough of a rotting motor-boat dragging a rotting rubber planter down the inlet. To the girl's imagination the inlet seemed a lusting mouth, the coiling river a throat. Her eyes followed the disappearing motor-launch. When she turned around her gaze was flinty.

"Dangerous? Perhaps it is. It looks rather—awful. But I won't accept your hint and run away on the next mail boat." Her glance smarted with scorn. "If you gentlemen are afraid of the danger, I'm not. I'll go alone."

BRADSHAW, the gaunt Kelantan naturalist, rose and dropped a kindly hand on the girl's arm. "We appreciate your desire to find this man you love," he said gravely. "Coming way out here from the States by yourself was a brave thing to do. But can't you see how hopeless it is? The man came nine years ago. Neither Schneider nor I were here then. Last night, as you asked us to, we made inquiries. Nobody would recall such a man. A rather tall white man about thirty years old? Dark hair? The natives could only shrug. They were exploiting iron and tin here at that time, and rumors of gold had brought many foreigners. A score of white men had stopped off; gone inland. Some had returned and drifted away. Some had disappeared. And nine years is such a long time. Perhaps thirty engineers have been here since then, and drifted away. And the scar you said he had on the palm of his right hand—a hopeless clue. Too difficult to notice. As for those mines in there, it's impossible that he'd have stayed. They've been deserted for over two years, I believe."

"But he may have gone farther inland. There's a colony in there. They told me white men had been living there. Planters, and men from the mines. Or he may have gone north. Or he may still be up that river—sick, penniless, ashamed to come out—"

"But my dear young lady," explained the naturalist patiently, "my friend has described the sort of jungle it would be necessary to travel through. For almost three years nobody has ventured that far in. In the first place it is believed that the white colony in there has scattered northward over the mountains. Of that I don't know. But everybody knows and fears the murderous renegade and his band of killers who range that territory—the dreaded Tok Jangut. The creature is rated with the most vicious crimes imaginable. He has pillaged the native towns without mercy, murdering, burning, torturing. Two white missionaries— a man and his wife—fell into his hands and were fiendishly tortured. The missionary managed to shoot his wife and escape from their camp. He came back only to spread a tale that would stir the police into action. His ears and the fingers of his left hand had been cut off. And there were other—and worse mutilations. And before he died he told a most horrible story, convincing the police that Tok Jangut was a maniac killer of the most dangerous sort. That was only eight months ago.

"And that's only a sample. For the last two years Tok Jangut has staged his little reigns of terror. He has eluded the police traps, and they have given up trying to smoke him out until they can send a large force in after him. The belief that he has left the region because he hasn't turned up, lately, is only guesswork. The renegade is crafty, and knows his country. He strikes and fades away like a ghost. The natives all carry arms, and don't dare go far from their villages. Armed natives present another danger." Bradshaw shook his head decisively. "You see, a journey inland would be impossible, what with the jungle and that marauding band of Tok Jangut. And even if you did get through there wouldn't be one chance in a thousand of finding the man. He may be dead."

THE GIRL brushed a tired hand across her forehead. She said: "I'm sorry. You don't understand after all. When his letters stopped coming four years ago, I—I knew he was not dead. Knew! It was hard to explain. At home I told nobody. They wouldn't have understood. One can't tell why; but one feels. He is alive. I know it as surely as I stand here. I'm going to him. He lives. I—I can tell."

Schneider, the beery Dutchman, ponderously stirred his vermouth and gin, and nodded heavily. "Ja! It is easy to understand those feelings to one who has lived in this country. A telegraph in the mind that can sense something ten thousand miles away. The Malays up the river know such things. The East has not forgotten its instincts; has not deadened the little feelings under its skin that warns of danger and tells of the unseen. The West has dulled its senses in its chase for money and bathrooms and fast automobiles. That is so. I can believe you.

"But I will tell you something hard. Instinct whispers to you that this man you love still lives. But it does not tell you how. No. It is unkind to say that men who come to the Orient sometimes forget. But they do. Everything." Schneider mopped his face, set down his glass, heaved to his feet and stood beside the girl. "Forget everything," he repeated, gently. "The East is a cruel mistress. She makes them forget. Even those they love."

THE GIRL'S lips tightened. She did not take her eyes from the swaying hedge of lush green which had already absorbed the rotting rubber planter in the rotting launch. "I know what you mean," was her low-voiced admission. "You mean he may have gone to pieces out here. Gone down. Started drinking, gambling, running with—with women. That's what my family said he'd do. He was too nervous, too intelligent and sensitive. They said a man as high-strung as John should never have gone to the Orient." Her fists were clenched at her sides when she swung around to face the two men. "Well, that's why I've come. He never would have come East had I protested. And I let him. In a way it was my fault. I thought it would be good experience for him to go away. He was brave and honest when he left. And even if he's sunk now, in this terrible place, he's brave and honest still. I don't care what he's done, I believe in him. I'm going to find him."

A glance passed between the two men. Bradshaw stepped to one end of the veranda and drew aside a rattan screen that had been shading their chairs from the westering sun. The girl, motioned to his side, looked out on the lane, ankle-deep with dust, that wandered towards a huddle of huts crowding the beach. The frame shanty of the Norwegian trader plastered with advertisements for Navy Cut Tobacco; the rusty iron wharf on the inlet side; the dowdy Continental Hotel; these were the only prints of western culture on a native scene. Bullocks and chickens and Chinamen and stray dogs and Malays moved languorously across the hot setting. Stirred by the breeze, the bell of a wat screened from view by a knot of jungle tinkled sweetly. A monkey quarreled on the lower limb of a casuarina tree that shaded the body of a ragged, scrawny man sprawled in the dust beside the lane.

Pointing with his pipe-stem, the naturalist asked the girl: "Do you see that beggar lying under the tree, there?"

A sob was startled from the girl's compressed lips. "Yes, I—I saw him there a little while ago. I thought he was a—a native. He's not white! That can't be a white man!"

"**THAT'S** what happens when they start to go," Bradshaw commented grimly. "Drunk, doped, shot to pieces with fever and alcohol and eating opium. Wrecked. That's a good example. That chap has been scrabbing in the dirt around here for the last year. They say he came up from Singapore. A rich planter at one time. And, now—not worth the effort to salvage. Goes off into the jungle and lives native. Bats around in the jungle long enough to pick up a couple of good pelts, then comes back here and plunges into a drunken, dopy wallow. Lower than a native. Why, he's torn himself into shreds. His own mother wouldn't know him now; wouldn't want to. You'd never want to find your man like that. Better never to see him again. You see how terribly futile your perilous journey might be."

"If he's like that," she said, voice low, "that's just why he should be found. A man can't kill his soul entirely—even that awful wreck out there in the lane. He's asleep. All he needs is something to wake him up. Who can tell? I could never run away, now, thinking I had left John behind as—as sunken as that creature under the tree. I must find him; prove him brave and honest. Even if he did go down. And—I'm going into the jungle. I'm going to reach the place where that white settlement was. I'll need the help of neither of you. A trader on the boat told me I could find a man here who knew the jungle trails well. He said I could get this man to take me if I paid enough. Well, I'll pay this man all the money he demands. The trader said his name was Skun, or Scrumm."

The tall naturalist sighed; stared at the rich green hedge of jungle, then at the man on his back beneath the tree. "Yes," he nodded. "He's the only man here who knows those trails well enough to lead a party. If you can't be discouraged from this mad trip, Schneider and I will have to go along. And this man will guide. He's the beggar stretched under the tree, there. And his name isn't Scrumm. It's Scum."

LATE afternoon; and they had abandoned the coiling river to follow the tangling jungle trail. Poking their way in a sampan up that sluggish stream had been bad enough, but following the path along its jungly shore was worse. For perhaps a mile the trail meandered with the water-course, then lost itself in a jungle bottom as evil as the Curse of Cain. On every hand stretched rotting mangrove swamp, thickets of dead trees, decaying underbrush, putrifying vegetal growth sinking in black bog. Clumps of thorny palm, klubi, and durian and bamboo, weighted with fungi, flourished in the mud. Decayed surface-roots clutched from green and stinking pools. Treacherous wallows of inky muck that smelled of age-old rot beguiled unwary feel and surrounded stagnant ponds crowded with crocodiles. Mattings of hanging vine clung and fed on every tree; and from this stew of green life and black death, simmering in the tropic sun, steamed a dismal, malarial mist as thick as fog.

Through this vicious maze, the man named Scum led the way. Limping along at even pace, a new Saint-Etiennes rifle in the crotch of his arm, eyes seldom leaving the ground before him, he followed a puzzled path with the sureness of a native. Only when the others floundered in the muck behind, and were forced to rest, would he halt his march. Then he would shift his knapsack, set down his rifle, and mop sweat from his haggard cheeks. Occasionally he would remove his sun-helmet, and stand turning it in his fingers, studying its broad band. New and white, it provided eloquent contrast to the rags fluttering on his rangy frame. He would look at the helmet as if surprised at the novelty of owning it. Then he would let his knotty fingers tap down the barrel of his gun.

HE HAD refused to lead the party at first. When Bradshaw had approached him with the idea he had snivelled an oath at the naturalist; cursed him as a fool. Why'd they have to keep picking on him? Why didn't they mind their own damn business and leave him alone? When he had been made to under-

stand that the naturalist was in earnest, his surprise was great. Would he guide them into that lousy jungle an' get hisself hacked to curry by a gang of renegades? He wouldn't do nothing for nobody, anyhow, an' he certainly wouldn't be damn fool enough to do that. Might be drunk, but he wasn't crazy. An' they could get t'hell away from him.

This—until the girl had produced a sheaf of five-pound notes, and begged him. The begging had made him sullen, but the notes had won. Money would buy many things. It would buy an endless round of drinks and dopes when the journey was over. It had bought the bottle of brandy which—breaking his promised intent to remain sober—he had sneaked into his kit. It had purchased the new Saint-Etiennes and the sun-helmet.

The helmet and gun pleased him, and so he would study them when he stood at rest. Sometimes he would beckon Bradshaw's Malay boy, Isa, to his side, and engage him in low-voiced, terse consultation. Seldom did he glance at the others grouped behind him. Only once had he spoken to them—surly words to the effect that they make as little noise as possible. When he thought they should be rested, he would shoulder his rifle and limp forward without a word.

Isa followed close on his bare heels. The little Malay was uneasy, and made no bones about the fact. His round and usually too placid face had been disturbed into unhappy wrinkles. His black eyes, beneath a shock of straight black hair, peered nervously at every darkening thicket. By the nervous way he would jerk up his feeble old LePage shotgun when a frog croaked suddenly from some slimy pool, he kept the party in a chronic state of jumps.

"By lieb' Gott!" ejaculated Willy Fat, Schneider's Chinese boy, when Isa had whipped up his gun for the fiftieth time. Willy Fat was usually staggered by his ability to swear in English and German, and had to tickle his ear by repeating the phrase a dozen times. Now he was angered into verbal parsimony. He gestured his antiquated Henry rifle and threatened in excellent dialect to shoot off the Malay's scalp the next time he lifted his gun—a threat backed up by a grim look from Schneider.

The girl followed Schneider's China boy, and some distance behind the Dutchman and the naturalist brought up the rear. Both were armed with Maynard rifles from the naturalist's gun rack—as was the girl—and both were far more vigilant than an observer might have suspected.

"IF THAT devil up ahead leads us into trouble," Bradshaw whispered to his companion, "my first bullet goes into his carcass. I'm marking this trail so we can back-track, an' don't you forget it. I've got Isa on the job, too. But the crazy idiot is scared to death. Malays are all on pins and needles when it gets

dark in the jungle. The poor fool will give us all the nerves. I tell you, Schneider, this is one of the maddest things I've ever been forced into in my life. I wish to God we'd made the girl go back home."

The Dutchman shrugged. Sweat leaked down his jowls, and his jacket was soaked beneath the pack across his shoulders. "What else could we do but come?" he panted. "Of course it is madness. But the girl—Herr Gott!—did ever you see one more determined? She will find this man or die, I am thinking. Ja! She would have come alone."

"We couldn't let her do that. That's the truth. But I certainly tried to change her mind. I only hope we get out of this alive, and see her back to the coast."

"It is all a madness," agreed Schneider. "It is crazy. It is love. *Himmel!* Love will do anything. Do you see her eyes when she speaks of this man? And there is faith. Already she expects to find him run to ruin like that jackal up ahead. And she wants to bring him back. It is foolish, that. It is nothing sane. Faith and love—that is madness. Ja! But she is a brave one, too."

The naturalist snarled. "That's a woman for you. Going through hell-fire for the sake of some skunk. It's love an' courage and all that. And this woman has a lot of it. But it's a lot of damned foolishness, too. A lot of copy-book sentiment. Lover comes to the Orient and goes to the devil. Girl comes out to find him and reclaim his soul—bring him back to manhood. This girl is drugged with sentimental bosh. If this man we're trying to locate is still alive—which isn't likely—the chances are he's living with a native and chewing betel-nut like that rotter Scum. A person who thinks they can reclaim these derelicts is a fanatic."

Bradshaw smiled bitterly. "Moving picture stuff. And I suppose we'll have to drag around these swamps in the teeth of a renegade who'd be only too glad to string us up over a bonfire—until this nonsense is sweated out of her, or she gets malaria. Then we'll pack her off to the States. She'll have been on her crusade, and'll be satisfied. And we'll be dosing with quinine, and offering prayers of thanks that we're still alive."

A grudging laugh escaped him. "She sure is courageous, though, at that. Imagine coming out here alone and batting off into the jungle with a strange gang of men. Only an American girl would think of such a thing. It's sporting, all right. Whew! This place would take the tuck out of an old-timer. And she acts like a veteran."

Schneider wagged his head. "That is love, my friend."

AND SO they marveled and marched through the mud, and could not but express admiration for the slim figure ahead of them. They were in for it. They would make the best of it, and see her through.

She was, indeed, keeping up like a veteran. Frightened as she must have been by the poisonous aspect of her surroundings, she kept her steps unflinchingly to the trail; dragged through slough and brush and creeper-woven thicket without complaint.

She had insisted on shouldering her own pack and gun. She wore high leather boots, twill breeches and the shooting-jacket Bradshaw had given her; and she carried the gun in a manner that spoke a familiarity with hunting. She was tired, but never lagged. Her eyes, shadowed by her sun-helmet, constantly sought the low ridge of hills dimly visible to northward—the hills that cradled the tin mine where the man she sought had last been heard of.

ON THE verge of sundown it rained, a lashing tropical downpour that drenched the travelers to the skin, made of the pestilential jungle bottom a morass, and brought a plague of leeches and fevery steam. As abruptly as it had started, the rain stopped. The jungle sweltered under a setting ball of molten steel.

Single file the little column wove its way through a dripping, vapor-clouded swamp, across a marshy brake to the edge of a clump of camphor where the choking undergrowth gave way to high ground carpeted with tall grass. Here was a deserted hut leaning in semi-ruin among the trees. Its sagging roof of thatched nipa-palm smoked under a shaft of sunlight. Its dark entrance breathed a musty odor that warned of mud and snakes.

Scum motioned Isa and Willy Fat to deposit their packs at the hut door. By that time the girl, the Dutchman and the naturalist had come up. Tilting his helmet over his eyes, Scum turned towards them with a leer. Avoiding the girl, he limped to Bradshaw's side.

"Y' c'n camp here," he muttered, poking a thumb at the hut. "Pitch yer tent inside th' house. Rake it over fer snakes, first, an' rats. An' don't make no big fires." His shifty eyes gave a hurried glance towards the girl. "Is she still set on headin' into them hills? Cos it ain't so healthy in there fer nobody. I'm tellin' you." His fingers plucked nervously in his ragged beard. "I'm tellin' you that this here Tok Jangut is in them uplands, an' I ain't so anxious to lose my hide, see? He'd like nothin' better than t' git his bloody hooks in us. Ho-ho! Then we'd do a dance, I'm tellin' you—" He broke off with a spasmodic coughing that brought tears to his eyes and a spot of color to his yellow cheeks.

The Dutchman grabbed Scum's arm. "You rat!" he growled, in a voice calculated not to reach the girl. "My friend and me wouldn't put it past you to betray us into the hands of Tok Jangut. Gott, no! And let us tell you now, that if you play us double we will jab our first two bullets into you. Ja! Do you understand?"

Scum yanked away. "Yah!" he sneered, showing his black teeth. "Maybe I wouldn't be so bloody sorry t' see you two git quartered by Tok Jangut. But I ain't a fool. He'd do fer me, too. Ever since he showed up aroun' here two years ago he ain't showed mercy to none as he's caught. It ain't that I'm lovin' a hog Dutchman an' a New England prig naturalist none. But I'm gettin' my own skin outa here. Then I gets my money an' y' c'n all be damned!"

BRADSHAW was about to make an angry retort when the girl stepped forward to join them. Her face was flushed, rouged with a touch of sunlight. Her eyes were bright, as she said: "Don't you think we'd better set up camp? We're all tired. And I overheard you quarreling. I'm sure we won't need to be afraid that Mister—uh—Scum won't do the right thing by us." She smiled at him. "You didn't join us at tiffin this noon. Won't you eat with us to-night?"

The invitation startled him. Keeping his eyes on he ground, he thrust his hands in his belt, twitched nervously, and mumbled refusal. Her presence embarrassed him. Whenever she was near he would keep his face turned away, hitch his shoulders, shift uneasily from one foot to the other. Now he hung his head and glared at his distorted feet.

"Eat by myself," he muttered ungraciously. And when she walked away, he turned on the naturalist. "What's she wanta go into them hills fer?" he coughed.

"I told you before we started," Bradshaw snapped. "If you'd keep sober once in a while, you'd know. She's trying to find this man who came out here. This man she loved—"

"Eh!" Darting a furtive glance at the girl, Scum swore huskily to himself. A curious glow came to his sunken eyes, and he brushed a trembly hand across his lips. Abruptly he grabbed up his kit, and started to limp towards a nearby glade overrun with rattan. "I'm campin' in here," he called over his shoulder. "An' in th' mornin' we gets goin' early." He lurched about. The colored twilight caught a strange twist to his sin-pocked face. On the point of speaking, he thought better of it, sneered, and plunged into the underbrush.

NATURALIST and Dutchman stared after him. In the west a blood-red disc sunk slowly behind the hills. Sultry night, rolling down from the east, was heralded by a vanguard of bats that whisked and zigzagged through the tinted dusk. Hard by in the jungle a hornbill chattered its shuddery laugh, to be answered by a chorus from the frog legions deep in the swamp. Schneider patted the butt of his rifle.

"Herr Gott!" he whispered to his companion. "This is not nice, my friend. That dope-eating Scum: there was something in his face—did you see? Something. Ja! And these jungles—"

Bradshaw nodded towards the hut. The girl was helping Willy Fat unpack a kit of cooking utensils. Isa, the Malay boy, was busy patting down the earth at the base of a little stick set before the hut door. A little stick on which fluttered a white rag.

"Isa's stuck up a flag to ward off evil," the naturalist consoled. He pointed to the hills arching against the northern horizon— hills mysterious in the falling dark. "With a scurvy derelict for a guide, a girl to look out for, an' a gang of murdering renegades in the offing we may have plenty chance when we reach those hills to try out Isa's charm."

As he spoke the night drank up the twilight at a gulp. And in the jungle not three miles away a humpbacked little Selangore Jacoon, armed with kris and blow-pipe, was speeding through the darkness as fast as his short, ugly legs could carry him. Speeding through the darkness for the hidden camp of Tok Jangut, with the news that a party of white men and a girl was heading into the hills.

A STEEP cliff jutted above a deep ravine that had been knifed out of the jungly slope, and its overhanging ledge formed the roof of a spacious cave where were a score of men squatted around a guttering fire. Flame-glow tossed witchlike shadows across the back wall of the cavern, brought out in fierce relief the features of those crouched around the fire, shone on the bulging, starey eyes of the corpse that hung by its thumbs in a gloomy corner. Fantasmal rain, falling in the darkness, draped a misty curtain over the mouth of the cave. The jungle without dripped and splashed; and a humid wind snatched tendrils of smoke from the flame, and gently swung the body of the hanging dead.

With shrill word and eloquent gesture, a humpbacked little Jacoon, squatting close to the fire, was telling a story. He looked a gnome crouching there, and his companions, listening avidly with mouths split in unholy grins, demons summoned from some foul Gehenna. Not the largest of those twenty, but certainly most vicious to the eye, was the man hunched beside the humpbacked story-teller. Matted gray hair fell in tangles down his brow. A bushing gray beard masked his mouth. Shrunken, dotted by the pock of sin, his face was made wholly diabolical by a kris-slash that tore out the corner of his right eye and left the eye bloodshot, ghastly red. As he listened to the Jacoon's story he stroked his beard with a powerful, tattooed hand; grunted brutishly; spat. One seeing the stabbing, insane glitter of his good eye would realize how he won the deference of those scoundrels about him. In it was a glitter as iced and cruel as that in the eye of a crocodile.

When the Jacoon had finished, this bearded ruffian jumped to his feet and yanked a slim dagger from his ragged sarong. "To the death of the white men!" he roared. His expression was that of a madman. "To the death of the white men! To a cave full of loot! And may the girl be beautiful to the sight!"

Nineteen voices shouted assent. Nineteen knives gleamed in upraised fists. The corpse hanging by its thumbs turned slowly in the sibilant breeze.

RAIN had fallen, for the greater part of the day. The sluicing downpours quit only to permit a blinding sun to broil the jungle with a stifling, gaseous heat. Dank mists clouded the creeper-choked, watery trails. The jungle bottom, flooded, mucky, alive with leeches and snakes, breathing fevers, was a veritable slough of despond.

All day the little column had slogged at snail pace through the green maze. Scum, a mud-splattered, tattered, gasping scarecrow, had limped in the lead. There had been alcohol in his eye at daybreak, and a haunted, hunted look. Neither the naturalist nor the Dutchman failed to mark the way he avoided the girl, keeping as far as possible ahead of the party.

"He's ashamed," Schneider had said. "That is so. He senses the decency of her. Ja. When she looks at him he shrinks and tries to hide that rotten face of his. She has been kind to him and he cannot understand, maybe. This morning he says to me, 'She is a brave woman. She should be made to go back.' He had been drinking, I think. It is the alcohol that keeps strength in those skinny limbs. And he is uneasy."

Bradshaw had declared: "Th'rotten beach-comber! I wouldn't trust him out of my sight for a second. I hope when we reach this tin mine and the girl finds nothing she can be made to go back. A hundred times I've told her it was a hopeless task to find this man. Nine years ago he came, and was thirty years old then. She wouldn't know him now—if he's alive. I tell you, Schneider, we've got to make her give up this fool chase. We've got to turn back from the mine."

And now they had gained the shadow of the hills. Higher ground hardly improved the going, for rivulets of water, creeping down the slopes, spread muck under foot. The humidity was strangling. The underbrush stank and steamed in the rain. Scum broke trail through a thicket of clumpy bamboo to follow a path Bradshaw recognized as an old elephant track. The two coolies, weighted with their heavy packs, staggered in the mud. Isa had begun his frightened peering at shadows again, and from time to time nervously jerked up his gun. His uneasiness filled those behind him with apprehension.

"Gott!" whispered the Dutchman. "I begin to feel like a rotten devil with a long knife hid behind every bush. That Tok Jangut—I cannot get him out of mind."

"Nor I," growled the naturalist. "The girl hasn't the slightest idea of the danger she's in, or what she's up against. It's a wonder we've gotten this far. Look: Scum has stopped and is beckoning to us."

STANDING atop a knoll where the underbrush cleared and rain beat freely on his wretched figure, the beach-comber motioned to the others. As the girl hastened to his side he ducked

his head and turned towards Bradshaw. "There," he mumbled.
He pointed a thumb. "There's th' tin mine. Ain't been nobody
in here for months."

For the girl it was a heart-straining moment. Only the tight
lines drawn from the corners of her mouth exposed her inward
agitation and disappointment. For the mine was nothing more
than a weedy ditch some five feet deep, a heap of gravel long
overgrown with grass, a tin smelter shed with caving roof and
walls devoured by red rust. A broken water-wheel, resembling
the skeleton of some strange animal, lay in the grass beside the
ditch. A mound of tin cans and rum bottles guarded the door
of the shed. This was the surviving monument of the engineer
who had come out to lick the East.

As the girl, wordless, stared, the clouds broke overhead, and
blatant sunshine flooded the dismal picture; drank at the muddy
puddles in the ditch. A score of krah monkeys began to chide
the visitors from their perch in a tree behind the shed. The
jungles whispered.

Bradshaw watched the girl, guessing what was in her mind.
No doubt her engineer had written of brave accomplishment
in this lonely hole; of foiling the jungle; of courageous engineering feats. She had pictured him commanding scores of coolies,
uncovering vast mineral deposits, opening up the dead back-
lands, pioneering. And now his only works disclosed a five-foot
hole, a rusty shed and a mound of cans and rum bottles.

"THE SHED," she said slowly. "Perhaps there is some trace
there. Something that would tell us where he had gone. And if
we find nothing here—we must push on. On to that settlement.
I must find him."

"Look here," said the naturalist with some asperity. "We can't
go farther than this. We'll investigate this mine, and then the
sensible thing to do will be go back. You can see for yourself
this place has been abandoned for months. Just—"

"I will go on," insisted the girl, "until I find someone who
knows or knew of him. Someone must have known him. That

scar on his hand ought to—" Suddenly she turned on Scum. "I never thought to ask you. They tell me you've lived in these jungles. Think! Perhaps you've seen him. There was a broad scar on the palm of his right hand. Shaped like a letter 'S,' and running from his thumb to the little finger. Perhaps you've—"

The man lowered his eyes. His fists clutched his rifle tightly. "No," he muttered sullenly. "I—I never knowed of no such man."

But when she left his side to run over to the door of the shed, she did not see the stricken look that had come to his face. She did not see him snatch Bradshaw by the sleeve; hear his croaking voice. Isa and Willy Fat were poking their guns into the shed door before her, and she failed to witness the little scene on the knoll.

"SCAR?" Scum's words clicked through his blackened teeth. His voice was hoarse. "Did I hear 'er say scar? On th' right palm! Like a letter 'S'? My God!" He was clutching his rifle so tightly that his knuckles showed white. Beneath dirt and scars the skin of the face showed pale blue. His lips faltered. "I—quick!" he stammered. "What's her name? An' what's th' name of this bloke she's tryin' to find?"

"Lieber Gott!" panted Schneider. "What is it you know? And—"

"Her name," Bradshaw explained hurriedly, "is Emily Rand. The engineer she's hunting is named Montgomery. John Montgomery."

"You mean," husked Scum—and his eyes glowed as if they watched some appalling scene that the others could not see—"you mean she come way out here huntin' this—this engineer, name of Montgomery. Way out here. I—w'y—" He coughed, shuffled, hitched his shoulders; and there was panic in his voice as he poked his gaunt face into Bradshaw's and snarled: "She's gotta turn back from here, see? Gotta! She won't never find nobody out here. I know these jungles like a book. Th' man—nobody ain't here." He broke off speech, and nodded towards the underbrush screening the foot of the slope they had just climbed. "Somethin' movin' down there. I'm gonna see."

"*Himmel!*" swore the Dutchman under his breath, as he watched Scum limp hurriedly away. His moon-round face squirmed. "He done that to escape from us. He is upset. I think so! Bradshaw, did you see him when you spoke those names? Green he went. Green. Ja! As if he had been hit in the stomach."

The naturalist stood as if petrified. Bright sunshine, filling that little clearing in the jungle with golden light, made jewels of the sweat-drops coursing down Bradshaw's cheeks. His voice was wooden, as he said: "Lord! It can't be. And yet—he's never looked her square in the eye. And when we told him those names, told him about that scarred hand it almost knocked him down. Looked as if he'd been knifed in the back. I—great heavens! Schneider, you don't think that he—"

"He what!" The Dutchman sucked in a hot breath. "Herr Gott! I see what you mean. *Himmel!* You mean that Scum is the—"

Schneider's words were choked in his throat. From the green wedge of jungle at the foot of the slope sounded a sudden, sharp explosion. Spang! Echoes scampered among the ravines; birds rose from the thickets; monkeys fled squawking. A cottony smoke-puff sailed up into the sunshine; and a smouldering hole had appeared with magic suddenness in the peak of the Dutchman's pith helmet.

THERE rose a clamorous, baying chorus of yells, and the next instant a score of savage figures broke from the jungle screen bordering the elephant track. Scum, not forty feet from the oncoming pack, yelled and fired. Bradshaw and Schneider shrieked warning in the same voice. Isa screamed. Willy Fat screamed. "Tok Jangut! Tok Jangut!" Bradshaw shouted at the girl, and told her to hide in the smelter shed. Dropping behind the knoll, where Schneider was already sending a lance of lead down the slope, he flung rifle to shoulder. The Maynard jumped and spat fire. A big yellow man who had sprung at Scum with upraised kris went stumbling to his face. Laboring his Saint-Etiennes as he ran, Scum fled up the slope, and dropped beside the naturalist.

"Hold 'em!" he wailed. "Keep 'em on the elephant track. Don't let 'em get into th' mine clearing!"

Their rifles whanged, and the tin smelter shed behind them sent the echoes banging. Bullets whistled over their helmets, and rattled like hail against the shed wall. Isa came crawling forward to tell that a bullet had found the forehead of Willy Fat and gathered him to his ancestors. Squatting beside the naturalist he howled out the news—and the moment he finished his recital was flung sprawling with a bullet in his throat. Blood squirted through his teeth as he writhed in the mud. Schneider turned a doughty face toward the shed.

"We got to get off this knoll. Quick! Back to the shed!"

A RATTLE of gunshots sounded behind them. The girl was shooting. They could see her crouching behind the mound of cans and rum bottles, loading and firing like a veteran. Her bullets drove into a rattan thicket left of the knoll, and a frenzied cry of anguish proved her shots unwanted. Yelling encouragement, Bradshaw crawled to the shelter of the gravel pile near the ditch. Schneider and Scum followed, raking the crest of the knoll they had just abandoned with a withering fire. Willy Fat lay spraddled beside the ditch, his bland Oriental face, washed with blood and grinning with death, resembling a Middle Kingdom festival mask. Scum caught up the dead coolie's Henry rifle, and emptied it at a black head poking above the knoll. The black head vanished, but five more replaced it.

There was no stopping that furious rush. Bellowing and squalling, the attackers sprang up the slope. Burnished blades and gun-barrels glinted in the sun. Wet bodies, brown, black and yellow, glistened in the weaving smoke. Faces evil, with brass earrings, filed teeth, tattooed cheeks, flickery black eyes, dodged in the haze. Tongues of fire spouted from their guns, and a rain of bullets dug into the gravel pile.

Firing in desperate speed, Bradshaw hit a big Chinaman who had just leapt the knoll. Spinning on his heels, the Chinese whirled like a dervish and rolled into the ditch. Schneider plucked the eye from a demon-faced Negro with a neat shot; and Scum furrowed the scalp of a little humpbacked savage who had scurried around the ditch waving a kris. The humpback dropped as if smote by lightning, but his fall did not halt the eight brawny villains who charged behind him. Swinging kris and rifle, they dashed across the clearing.

Scum screamed to make himself heard. "Behind 'em! Tok Jangut!" His gun crackled and his bullets ripped over the head of a fearsome devil who was sprinting forward voicing bar-baric yells—a fearsome devil whose bushing gray beard tossed down his chest, whose tattered sarong fluttered as he ran. Matted hair tumbled over his face and partly hid the wounded eye that smouldered in his head like a live coal. In one hand he clutched a massive automatic, in the other a ponderous ax—a battle-mace that flashed fire in the sun. He screamed at the gang around him, and pointed at the smelter shed. Scum shouted: "He's seen th' girl!"

SCHNEIDER cursed, fighting to load his Maynard. Bradshaw had thrown down his rifle and was shooting, automatic at hip—spang! spang! spang! spang! A bullet knocked the helmet from his head, and a hurled dagger scratched his temple, drawing blood. Scum's Saint-Etiennes roared, the reports echoing as one explosion. The girl had fainted. The tall renegade swinging the mace was rushing towards the trash-heap sheltering her recumbent form. The knot of men surrounding him dealt a scorching fire at the three behind the gravel pile. At the same time another squad of ruffians charged from the bamboos on the other side of the smelter shed.

Schneider had those four under his sight, and felled three of them with the skill of an old army campaigner. The fourth chipped the Dutchman's shoulder with a fast shot, but never stopped his flow of oaths and bullets. Bradshaw, blinded with smoke and blood from the scrape on his temple, emptied his automatic to kill two of Tok Jangut's supporters; but the rash was not halted.

And then Scum was on his feet with a shrill cry. Swinging his Saint-Etiennes about his head as if it had been a malacca rod, he charged from behind the gravel. "You'll never get her!" he was screaming. "You'll never get her!" Like a maniac he went cycloning into that villainous crew, whipping his gun-butt. Surprised by his mad attack, those devils clustered around Tok Jangut faltered, wavered, then fell on him like a pack of wolves. Knives slashed at his haggard face. Guns spurted under his chin. Blood washed down his cheeks and naked arms. But he did not go down. He did not go down; and he waded through that screaming, clawing tangle as if it had been boiling surf. Gun-butt swinging, he smashed a path through until he reached the girl.

SHE HAD come to consciousness, and was huddled against the shed wall, hands pressed against her eyes. As Scum gained her side, Tok Jangut flung himself to the fore with upraised mace. Lashing out with all his might, Scum brought his gun-butt smashing hard across the renegade's mouth. Whack! The battle-ax fell to the ground. Blood pouring into his beard, the renegade went reeling into the gang behind him; staggered, stumbled, lurched to his feet, and fled screeching over the knoll and down the slope. The remainder of his band scattered like leaves in wind, dropping their weapons and dashing for cover.

Bradshaw and the Dutchman sent a shower of steel after them. The naturalist went thrashing into the underbrush, pumping bullets. Running hard, Scum gained the knoll. Bradshaw's dead Malay boy lay there, and, in passing, Scum stopped to grab Isa's fallen gun. The little humpbacked savage whom Scum had dropped at the start of the fight rolled on his side as Scum went by. Raising himself on an elbow, he jabbed a tiny blow-pipe to his lips. His brown cheeks puffed out. Scum groaned; flung around and fired the old LePage in the humpback's face. Then he reeled down the slope, and plunged into the underbrush where Tok Jangut had vanished.

Schneider, close on Scum's heels, heard the LePage bark twice more. Bradshaw's Maynard exploded near at hand, then the Dutchman heard the naturalist calling out. A moment later and he came backing out of the underbrush, dragging the limp form of Scum after him.

"Help me!" he called to the Dutchman. "That damned savage stuck a poison dart into Scum's spine, and his right hand is blown off! Quick!"

TOGETHER they carried the groaning, bloody figure across the silent and gory mine clearing to the shade of the smelter shed. Already huge gadflies had found the bodies of the dead, and lusting vultures were wheeling high in the blue. Schneider's round face was pallid, and he stood shoving shells into his gun. Trembling, wide-eyed, white-faced, the girl stood with tight-clasped hands. Bradshaw knelt beside the wounded man. Scum's face was masked with blood, his crooked features twitching, his lips violet. The bandanna bound around his shattered right hand dripped and soaked from crimson to dark maroon. A thread of scarlet leaked from his twisted mouth.

"Tok Jangut—" he whispered, opening his eyes. "I—I got him. He won't get far. An'—an' they won't come back. But—th' poison dart got me. In th' back—an'—" His sunken eyes glowed, and he strove to lift his shoulders. "I—I say. Th' girl—is she all right?"

"She's safe," Bradshaw promised. And he could not restrain the words: "But look here! I saw you in there. You fired a shot at Tok Jangut, then put your hand over the mouth of your gun and fired again. I saw you do that, and what—"

It was the girl who made answer. Dropping on her knees, she clutched Scum's beaten, tousled head to her bosom; sobbed as she patted and smoothed his tortured forehead. "I know. You did it because you didn't want me to know. You shot off your scarred hand so I would never recognize—O John! John! I wondered when I first saw you if—John! I knew! I knew you'd keep brave and fine at heart. The bravest of all." Her cheeks glistened. "Always brave and fine," she repeated. "You saved us all, John. The—the bravest—"

"Lieber *Gott im Himmel!*" groaned the Dutchman.

Clasped in the girl's arms, the dying man smiled. "Go home now," he whispered. "That's best. Go home. Safe. I—I'm done."

Bradshaw nodded at Schneider, and the Dutchman took the girl by the arm and gently led her away. The naturalist made a pillow of his jacket to ease the dying man's head; stopped low to catch the shadowy voice. The sunken cheeks were already smoldering with poisoned blood, the eyes squeezed shut. Bradshaw just managed to catch the whispered words: "My hand. Shot off. Done it fer her, see? Send her home. Done it fer her. Because—she—she was so damn square. So—so almighty game—"

Death drummed in the contorted throat.

The sunlight faded abruptly. It started to rain.

LATE afternoon sunshine sparkled on the restless waters of the bay, and tinted the plume of smoke that crawled down the horizon—the plume of smoke that marked the passage of the weekly mail boat heading for Rangoon. Bradshaw, the gaunt Kelantan naturalist, stood on the veranda step with an untouched stenger in his hand, attention divided between the boat dropping over the skyline and the fat Dutchman laboring hurriedly up the dusty road from town. Fat Dutchmen do not hustle through the tropic sun without unusual incentives. The naturalist wondered what brought his friend a-hurrying at siesta hour.

"Ho!" greeted Schneider, as he gained the veranda step, panting. Wiping his face, he dropped into a wicker chair and reached a practised hand for the whiskey decanter.

Nodding, Bradshaw dropped into a chair beside his visitor. It was easy to see something was troubling the beery Dutchman, and mightily. He drank a finger of whiskey with gusto; poured another. "Hot," suggested the naturalist by way of opening conversation.

"Hot as the devil," Schneider complained. His eyes sought the bay, and he fanned himself nervously. "Say," he asked. "That girl: Did she take the boat this afternoon? Is she gone?"

The naturalist pointed at the smoke-smudge going hazy on the horizon. "There she goes, old man. I saw her aboard, and she wanted me to thank you for all you'd done. At the burial, and all. She seemed quite reconciled, too, and happier than I'd ever seen her. Poor little thing, she certainly stood up under an awful strain. Her last words were to request that we water those flowers she planted for him, and the very last thing she said was, 'He was a man after all.' Schneider, there goes the whitest, gamest woman in all the world."

"You are right, my friend." The Dutchman nodded heavily. Then he brushed a hand across his cheeks, swung around in his chair, and dropped a hand on Bradshaw's knee. "Listen. *Himmel!* this is going to sound queer. But tell me, my friend. Did it not seem funny to you, the way—the way he shot off his hand there in the thicket?"

THE QUESTION surprised an exclamation from the naturalist. He stared at his friend with startled eyes. "Why, yes," he made reluctant admission. "But I suppose the poor devil thought he'd tear away the last mark to identify him. He knew he would die, from that dart in his back. And he didn't want the girl to ever know he'd become such a—a scarecrow. And—"

"But suppose he only wanted her to think he was this engineer she hunted," Schneider burst out. "Suppose he only wanted her to think she'd found her man. Then she'd go away and never come back. Ja! That would save her life, maybe. You remember what he said to you. 'I done it for her.' That is what he said. 'Because she was so game.' Herr Gott!"

"You mean," gasped the naturalist, "that you don't think Scum was Montgomery? That he shot off his hand to make her believe he was Montgomery, trying to hide his identity. That Scum was not—"

"This morning," announced Schneider, as if making an effort to change the subject, "the police brought in the dead body of Tok Jangut. I saw it down at the hotel. They had found him hiding, wounded, in a cave, and killed him. The body is at the hotel. Come."

ONLY one thing more would the Dutchman say, and he said it just as he and Bradshaw reached the hotel veranda. "Nobody must know. And remember, my friend, that Scum knew this Tok Jangut. Perhaps he had seen him in the jungle. Perhaps he had even belonged to his band. But Scum—was a man at the last. Ja! A man!"

And he did not speak again, but led Bradshaw into the hotel to the room where the corpse of Tok Jangut lay. That evening that body would be hung in public gallows so all could see the dreaded renegade was dead. Going over to the corpse, Schneider stooped and held to light the lifeless right hand. Gray of face, Bradshaw stared. There across the palm from thumb to little finger ran a broad white scar—a scar shaped like the letter "S."

ABOUT THE AUTHOR

AS A GUEST speaker at Pulpcon in Dayton, Ohio in July, 1986, I played the old Q. and A. game. I believe the opening of that game makes a good beginning for the present discussion of my fiction writing for the pulps.

Q. How and when did my fiction writing begin?

A. I have in my files the initial effort—a book entitled *The Devul and the Knight* [sic] written age five, hand-printed, hand-illustrated and hand-bound, price one cent (two copies, one remainder). The "K" circumflexed over the "night" was inserted by a brother ten years my senior. From the penny profit (from a sale within the family), I purchased a Mary Jane—taffy wrapped around a glob of peanut butter. Um.

Q. Then?

A. Shortly thereafter, I wrote, hand-printed, hand illustrated and hand-bound *Hawk Eye the Indian Boy* (two copies, price one cent, one remainder) which bought me another Mary Jane.

Q. And?

A. There followed a production entitled *The Sheriff of Red Roach Ranch*. ("Roach" was the spelling of my wicked older brother when I asked him if "Rock" was spelled with two "Ks." No matter.) I copied the spelling "Sheriff and "Ranch" from a book I was reading. Again, the one cent sale (leaving one remainder) paid for another Mary Jane.

Thus I conceived a notion.

Born was the idea that by writing I could eat.

That idea served as an apothegm for my subsequent career as a writer—a ruling not invariably a truism. As it eventuated there were times when I had Thanksgiving dinner at bottom of the totem pole at a hot dog stand.

However, I wrote many yarns for my high school magazine-an effort that caused an English teacher to suggest I submit a fiction effort to a magazine. Not overly optimistic, I knew I couldn't compete in a try for that day's top, the *Saturday Evening Post.* So I picked a pulp—*NorthWest Stories.* Luck! A check for $40.00! And a request for another story. This first story, "The Duel," would appear in the September 1926 issue.

That did it.

It was summertime, and I'd been a temporary P.O. employee peddling mail on a route on Long Island. With a high school buddy similarly employed, who shared room and board. And I had just carried a very heavy parcel-post package addressed to a "Tillie Tisswisser," 8,001 some local avenue at the end of the line. After lugging it an extra half mile, I discovered there was no such address. Belatedly suspicious, I pried open one corner of the package and exposed a cinder block. Which my pal had wrapped and mailed with a slew of cancelled stamps.

That would have done it if my check hadn't come that day with $40.00. "I quit! I just made a fortune!" I told them at the P.O. where I dumped the cinder block. (And I got even with my buddy by ducking out of our boarding house by letting my suitcase out of our bedroom window on a clothes line and leaving him stuck with the rent.)

Anyway, the $40.00 check started me on what eventuated as a career, writing for *Action Stories, Argosy, Short Stories* and *Adventure,* for such astute editors as Jack Byrne, Don Moore and, after the war (World War II), Burroughs Mitchell and Bud Hart. Of whom I still see Bud Hart—the others no longer among those present.

World War II pretty much killed most of the now extinct pulps. From paper shortage? I can't say. But many pulp writers faded away during the war. Among them, one of the best. Frederick Faust ("Max Brand"). I'm not certain, but I believe he may have been killed at Anzio.

Theodore Roscoe

If one finds some astonishing names among the early pulp editors some of the writers are equally surprising. In the early *Argosy-All Story.* Mary Roberts Rinehart, Octavus Roy Cohen, Zane Gray, E. Phillips Oppenheim, John Buchan. (Buchan, who wrote "The Thirty-Nine Steps," became Governor-General of Canada.)

ONE of the questions often asked me is how did I happen to write about an old veteran yarn-spinner who spun yarns about his service in the French Foreign Legion. In North Africa back in the early '30s I encountered on a street in Casablanca this old-time Legionnaire with hashmarks up to his elbow. He agreed to talk over wine at a *brasserie.*

He didn't wear the classic old-time Legion uniform-the button-back blue overcoat, white trousers, blue cummerbund, heavy desert-boots called *brodequins.* He wore an old artillery-man's outfit. But the square-brim *kepi* with the gold torch insignia was Legion.

Questioning him in my limping French, and struggling to comprehend his metaphors, I got a *formidable* story. Aside from obvious hyperbole and manifest adjectives, some of it was perhaps true.

Here was my prototype for Thibaut Corday. Which, of course, wouldn't be his right name. You could enlist in the Legion under any name you chose, and since his right name was Hyacinth Rastagouch, he chose Corday for what is called a *nom de guerre.* Which became your official name as a "Stepson of France."

Meaning you couldn't be extradited for a crime committed elsewhere—a fact, it was said contributed to the enlistment of numerous criminals using an alias. Who knows?

Because Frenchmen can't enlist in the French Legion, I had Corday say he was a Belgian. Or was it a Swiss? Anyway, the teller of my story attributed to Corday good English, partly translated.

Since his yarns were obviously mixtures of fact and fiction, I never presumed they would be taken seriously by the reader. And was surprised when several critics wrote to tell me the military tactics in this or that Corday tale were hokum. They were so intended to sound.

Incidentally, some Legion veterans in New York voted me an honorary member of the Veterans of the French Foreign Legion.

Actually, I never saw the Legion in combat. At a Legion H.Q. back in Sidi Bel Abbes, I was querying one of the officers. Apparently he thought I was planning to enlist. He shook his head at me with the comment: *"Discipline terrible!"* They followed the old rule, *"March qu creve."* "March or die." If a Legionnaire fell out, exhausted, in a Sahara march, they sent a sharpshooter back to kill him, and spare him from torture by desert tribesmen. But the Legionnaires I saw in action weren't risking their lives.

In Europe back then there was a saying. When the English conquer a country they build a custom house. The Germans build a fort. The French build a road. Back then (the '30s) the Legionnaires I saw in action were covered with not-very-glamorous dust, wielding picks and shovels building a road. Some of them in barracks slept in cots with the cot-legs in cans filled with water, to defeat scorpions. Their pay, if I recall correctly, afforded them a daily bottle of *pinard* (cheap red wine). Nothing so intriguing, colorful and lively as in such novels as *Beau Geste.*

So don't join the French Foreign Legion today. You'd get a plain khaki uniform, and risk only being bored to death.

Still, you'd learn one thing. Watch them, if chance occurs, on parade in France or on TV. There's no military outfit anywhere that can out-march their particular step.

ASIDE from the Foreign Legion, I most enjoyed writing for *Action Stories* a series about an adventurer named Peter Scarlet. There were at least 14 Peter Scarlet stories, beginning with "Jungle Joker" in the May 1927 issue of *Action Stories*. Other favorites were a tale entitled "On Account of a Woman" (*Adventure,* January 1936) and a tale for *Argosy,* "The Voodoo Express" (October 10,1931).

On another tack, I enjoyed writing a series for *Argosy* titled "Four Corners," which began with "He Took Richmond" in the June 5, 1937 issue of *Argosy.* These were adventures experienced by a youngster whose uncle was Sheriff in a small town about 100 miles from New York. One of the early Four Corners stories was "I Was the Kid With the Drum" (October 30, 1937)—a murder mystery. They used to have a kid aid the drummer by carrying in a parade the front end of a big base drum (guess where the body was concealed in a hurry by the murderer in this case). Of course, the drum seemed heavier than usual. And the drum-beat seemed more of a thump than the usual vibratory boom. The kid in the story didn't get it. But anyway the murderous drummer discovered he'd killed the wrong person.

In another "Four Corners" tale, I had a thief change his money into coins—loot he could bury in a well. Okay? But when he went back to safely get and spend this big bag of coins, he was trapped by the fact the silver dollars all bore the same date—the date of the robbery.

In one of my favorite Four Corners stories, "Frivolous Sal" (*Argosy,* July 17, 1937), the small town gentry were worried because it was rumored the young woman, so named (after a popular song), kept a diary. Fruitless efforts were made to get hold of it. In the end? Try to guess it.

I had a lot of fun writing "The Head," which appeared in *Short Stories,* December 10, 1932. As a stringer reporter, I had gone to Panama to investigate rumors of "White Indians" in the remote interior near the Colombian border. At a bar in Cristobal I asked the bar-keep if he'd heard of these Indians. Overhearing my query, a bar-fly character asked if I was interred in Jiboro Indians—the tribe that, through a mysterious process, boned, cured and somehow shrank human heads to the size of a baseball. (Origin of the term "head-shrinker" for a psychologist.) The bar-fly said he had one to sell, and produced what appeared to be a much-shrunken human head. As the Jiboro Indians actually beheaded their enemies and with incredible artsy-crafty skill created such curiosities, I was interested in the specimen handed me by the bar-fly. Ah! Only $300.00.

But the bartender, behind his hand, winked at me a negative signal. I didn't buy the head.

When the bar-fly indignantly took off with his allegedly shrunken head, the bartender advised me it was a fake, a monkey head fixed up to look human.

Later I saw an authentic shrunken head on display in another bar.

When World War II put an end to my pulp efforts, by good luck I sold *Only in New England*—a novel I'd intended for *Argosy*—to Scribner's. Surprisingly, it made the Literary Guild Book of the Month.

Thereafter, I wrote two Navy histories—*U.S. Submarine Operations, World War II* (1949) and *U.S. Destroyer Operations, World War II* (1953) which were published by the Naval Institute at Annapolis (and are still on the market). I also wrote *This is Your Navy* (1950) for service reading. This was followed by *The Web of Conspiracy* (1959), about the Lincoln assassination, which became a *DuPont Show of the Month* on TV in 1961. Of which, with a great deal of help from my devoted wife, Rosamond, got me going again in fiction.

Today I can't recall what some of these tall tales written 50 years ago were about. Maybe I should have written some of them under an assumed name. But when I wrote them I felt I should take my lumps if, compared to many of early *Argosy's* great writers, my efforts proved mediocre. And on the other hand, if some drew plaudits, I'd like to take a bow in person.

Brave, no?

THE ARGOSY LIBRARY ™

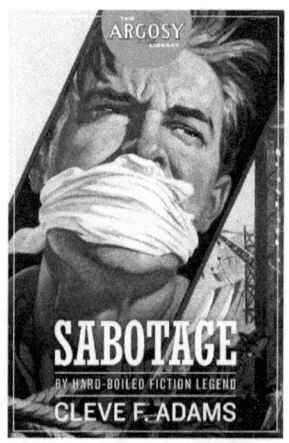

SABOTAGE
BY HARD-BOILED FICTION LEGEND
CLEVE F. ADAMS

CHAMPION OF LOST CAUSES
BY WILLIAM F. NOLAN
MAX BRAND

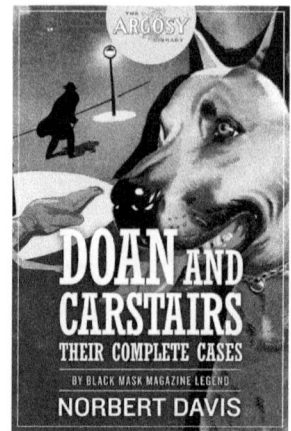

DOAN AND CARSTAIRS
THEIR COMPLETE CASES
BY BLACK MASK MAGAZINE LEGEND
NORBERT DAVIS

THE KING WHO CAME BACK
BY THE AUTHOR OF THE RAMBLER
FRED MacISAAC

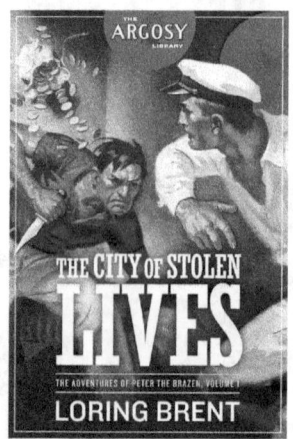

THE CITY OF STOLEN LIVES
THE ADVENTURES OF PETER THE BRAZEN, VOLUME 1
LORING BRENT

THE RADIO GUN-RUNNERS
BY SCIENCE FICTION LEGEND
RALPH MILNE FARLEY

BLOOD RITUAL
THE ADVENTURES OF SCARLET AND BRADSHAW, VOLUME 1
THEODORE ROSCOE

THE SCARLET BLADE
THE RAKEHELLY ADVENTURES OF CLEVE AND D'ENTREVILLE, VOLUME 1
MURRAY R. MONTGOMERY

SEMI DUAL
THE COMPLETE CABALISTIC CASES OF
THE OCCULT DETECTOR, VOLUME 2: 1912–13
J.U. GIESY AND JUNIUS B. SMITH

SOUTH OF FIFTY-THREE
BY THE AUTHOR OF THE TORCH
JACK BECHDOLT

SERIES 2 • AVAILABLE SPRING 2015